LOVE IN THE RAGGED MOUNTAIN RANGES

BARRINGTON BOOK THREE - A NOVELLA

SUSAN MACKIE

LOVE IN THE RAGGED MOUNTAIN RANGES

SUSAN MACKIE

For Gordon, my very own horse whisperer.
Miss you Dad.

Susan Mackie

1

Nik turned onto Copeland Road, the surface was old and pitted bitumen, and barely wide enough for one car. She flashed a bright smile at Lucy. 'Just a few minutes now, Luce. I can't wait to see it again.'

Concentrating on the rough and winding road, overhung with huge gumtree branches, Nik leaned forward. The day was already warm but turning onto the smaller road the temperature seemed to drop, just a little. The high peaks of the Barrington Tops loomed closer.

The road narrowed further, and she slowed the car to a crawl, while drawing in her breath. 'Funny, but it didn't seem this rough back in September.' She felt, rather than saw, Lucy glance at her. She was leaning forward too, and Nik risked a quick sideways look. Her daughter's usually pensive expression had lightened. She seemed almost eager to get there. A wave of relief washed over her. She was doing the right thing. For Lucy.

And for herself. This was a fresh start. Nodding, she told herself moving here was the right decision.

They passed a couple of narrow driveways, their entries obscured by large cedar trees, each with its own leaning letterbox.

'It should be the next one to the left. The old Copeland Courthouse, built in the eighteen eighties at the height of the gold rush.' Nik grinned across at Lucy, who smiled tentatively back. 'And it's ours now. Our home.'

'Stop, Mum. You've gone past.' Lucy turned in her seat, peering out her side window. Nik stopped and reversed slowly. 'Yes, there's the sign. It says Courthouse. Oh, the entrance is pretty isn't it?'

Nodding agreement, Nik paused. The sign Lucy had spotted was on an angle, the lettering worn, the paint faded. But the entrance was gorgeous, if a little overgrown. Large posts stood on each side of the driveway, a rusty iron gate swung back against the inside fence, the dirt and gravel driveway leading up to the high set building just visible through thick native foliage.

'It will need some work. Not just the house, but the whole block. Fences need repairing and this driveway will have to be graded and gravelled. But we're not in a hurry. We'll work out what needs doing the most and we'll start there.' Driving further in, the building came into view. They sat in the car for a moment, peering up at the house in front of them.

The old courthouse had been turned into a family home in the early nineteen hundreds and lived in by various families for over a century, some renovating and extending as they went. Nik knew the ground level had been a jail and quarters for courthouse staff in the early days. The upper level was split in two, with the courthouse itself at the front, and the magistrate's accommodation at the back. Several outbuildings squatted in the undergrowth, including the original stables that had been turned into cottage accommodation at some point. It was all a bit rundown. Heaps of potential though.

'Gold was discovered around here in the eighteen seventies, or maybe eighties. The real estate agent told me there were twelve pubs and about four thousand people in this valley then. That's why the courthouse is so big.' Nik had told Lucy this when she first found the property but said it again to remind herself that the history of the place, the valley and the buildings, was significant.

Lucy nodded, then opened her door and scrambled out. Nik did the same. Walking to the front of the car she slung an arm around her daughter's shoulders, giving her a quick squeeze. 'You'll help me plan this out, won't you Luce?' She kissed the top of Lucy's head as she spoke.

Tears came to Nik's eyes as Lucy leaned into her. Her voice a murmur. 'It's just us now, Mum. You and me. We can do this together. We don't need anyone else.'

'You're right. It's ours. We'll plan it together. But Luce, we will need help. We'll have to get tradespeople like an electrician, and maybe a carpenter or builder. And someone to grade the driveway. But they won't live here. It will just be us. Well, maybe some guests eventually when we have the bed and breakfast part ready.'

Lucy stretched and turned in a circle, long legs belying her tender years. 'I know. But it's ours. I like that it's ours.'

Walking toward the house, Nik glanced around. It was greener than last time, the drought had broken. Everything was overgrown, but that was easily fixed. There was a large yard in front, and she knew there was a fenced paddock behind and another to the side. Big enough for a pony, or maybe two. Lucy was horse-mad and hopefully she could find a quiet horse for her to begin.

THE DAY WORE ON AS THEY UNPACKED THE CAR, CRAMMED WITH kitchen items and clothes. The removal truck should have arrived around lunch time, but it was almost three and there was no sign of it.

After a good look through both levels of the house, they decided they would live upstairs themselves. The ground floor was already set up for separate living, with a small kitchen and bathroom, two bedrooms and a lounge and living area, perfect for guests. Doors that led out from the rear opened to a small courtyard, the paving neat, the original hand-made bricks laid in intricate patterns. It would be excellent accommodation once she upgraded the kitchenette and bathroom. Fresh paint inside and out and the right furniture and it would be ready. They would focus on that first.

Upstairs needed more work. There had been so many renovations, alterations, wallpaper, and paint over the years, that it needed to be brought back to the original timber boards before contemplating anything further. It also needed a new kitchen and bathroom and maybe an ensuite. But it was liveable, and downstairs should be renovated first.

About to head out to the cottage that in years past was the stables, they heard the removal truck struggling along the driveway in low gear. The high back of the truck was dragging through the tree branches and Lucy cried out when a large branch snapped off and bounced off the side of the truck, hitting the ground before rolling under the back wheels and stopping the vehicle altogether.

'Wait here Luce.' Nik strode forward to meet the driver as he climbed down from the cab. His face was florid, and he wiped the back of his neck with a large cloth as he stomped towards her. His passenger, a younger, fit-looking man had walked to the back of the truck and was trying to lift or pull the branch out, but it was firmly stuck, the truck wheels sitting squarely on it.

'You didn't mention the trees over the driveway when we quoted this job. I'm going to need either a tow out, or someone with a chainsaw to cut that branch up and get it out from under the truck. Either way, we are not going to get your furniture unloaded before dark and you will have to pay accommodation for me and Jimbo.' Hands on hips, he glared at Nik.

'I'm sorry Dave, I didn't recall the entrance being this over-grown when I was here last.' Nik smiled, hoping if she stayed polite and friendly, he might calm down. She glanced behind her to see if Lucy was nearby, but she had vanished. She hated confrontation; Nik knew she would stay out of the firing line.

'Look Nicola, I realise it's not your fault, but we need to get some help here quickly or we'll lose light altogether. And the truck is blocking anyone getting in or out now.' Somewhat mollified, Dave turned back to look at Jimbo still pulling at the tree branch. He shouted, 'It's no good Jimbo, we need a chain-saw. It's too big!'

'Can you try backing over it, do you think Dave?' Nik felt sweat beginning to trickle down between her shoulder blades.

She wiped her arm across her eyes, her shoulder length dark bob curling at the ends in the heat and humidity.

Sighing, Dave nodded at Jimbo. 'I'll have another go at backing over or rocking back and forth to see if I can get the wheels off it. Stand back though in case it snaps or flicks out at you.' Dave climbed back into the cabin of his truck, while Jimbo moved to one side.

The truck revved as it was thrown into reverse, the wheels spinning on the solid timber. He then put it in gear and tried moving forward. Again, the wheels spun. Several attempts to move forward and back made no progress.

'Damn.' Nik pulled her phone from the back pocket of her jeans, turning her back on the truck, hoping to google some help. She had no idea if there would be a tow truck in the area and if there was any hope of finding someone with a chainsaw on Boxing Day. The service was only one bar, and she struggled to get any search results. Perhaps she could call the real estate agent, Ben Evans, or his offsider Harriet Russell. She tried Ben's number, but it rang out.

'Hey there. Perhaps I can help.' The deep voice was right behind her. Spinning around the phone flew from her hand, landing at the feet of a man she could only describe as a cowboy. Hat pulled low, collared shirt with sleeves rolled up to large biceps, broad chest, faded jeans and work boots. She glanced at his face, partly shaded by his hat, squinting a little to read his expression.

'Excuse me.' He removed his hat with his left hand, holding his right hand out. 'I'm Robbie Stewart. Live just up the road, saw the truck, ah, wedged in the driveway. Thought I might be able to help.' Reaching down, he scooped her phone from the ground and handed it over with a lopsided grin. Her fingers touched his as she took it from him, bringing a flush of warmth to her face.

Smiling tentatively, Nik shook his hand. The warmth receded from her face but settled somewhere lower. Ignoring it, she mentally shook her head, then looked him in the eye. His grin broadened, deepening the laugh lines around his eyes.

'Nicola Reid. Nice to meet you. Thank you. Yes, we need some help. Branch came off and is wedged under the back tyres. Dave, the removalist, hasn't been able to budge the truck either forward or back. Do you know of a tow truck in the area?' She sucked in some air as Robbie strode toward the truck and waited as Dave climbed out.

They spoke for a moment, then Robbie squeezed past the side of the truck, heading toward the road. Nik walked over to Dave.

'Is he calling a tow truck?'

'No love. He's got a chain saw in the back of his ute, parked at the entrance back there. He's going to cut up what he can get too, then we might be able to shift the truck a bit.'

'Oh. Good. Well, that's very nice of him.' Nik turned around to check on Lucy. She was up on the veranda of the top floor of the house. She gave her a wave. Lucy smiled and waved back. Good. Best she was out of the way.

Robbie reappeared with a chainsaw and began cutting the timber up, with Jimbo moving the heavy pieces and stacking them to one side. Trying to relax, Nik told herself at least she'd have some firewood when the weather cooled. She stepped forward to offer help, but Dave touched her on the arm. He was leaning against the front tyre, lighting a cigarette. 'Let the young blokes do it. They look fit enough.'

Nik moved forward when Robbie crawled under the truck,

chainsaw in hand. 'Is he going to use that thing under there? Laying down?' She was incredulous. Jimbo just grinned and crawled under behind Robbie, pulling the large pieces out as they were cut up.

Twenty minutes from start to finish and Robbie was standing back, the chainsaw at his feet. 'Try to edge forward now Dave but turn the wheel a bit as you go. I think if we can get one side over, the other will be easy. We'll have some traction on the driveway.' He picked up the chainsaw and moved back a few paces, touching her lightly on the arm to indicate she step back too.

Dave revved the engine and edged forward, spinning the wheels again. He threw it in reverse and edged backwards, then back into gear, the truck surging forward, on a slight angle. A loud crack signalled that the end of the branch had broken under the tyres; the vehicle moved forward again, rolling effortlessly over the last piece.

'Yay!' Nik fist-pumped the air as Dave grinned from the cab of the truck, a cigarette dangling from his mouth. Jimbo leapt forward to pull the last two pieces to the side. The truck came in and turned side on to the house, barely stopping before Jimbo had the rear doors open and the ramp pulled down.

'You need to tell us where you want everything, love. I don't fancy finishing in the dark.'

Looking up, Nik knew there would only be an hour or two of daylight left, so she resigned herself to just getting everything unloaded as quickly as possible. She looked around to thank Robbie, but he and his chainsaw had vanished, his vehicle no longer at the end of the drive, so he must have left. She should have thanked him properly or at least offered him a cold drink.

Dashing into the house, she found Lucy at the top of the

stairs. 'Do you want to help, Luce? Are you able to show Dave and Jimbo where everything should go?'

Lucy chewed on a fingernail and shook her head. Taking a breath, Nik walked up the stairs and hugged her tightly. 'It's okay, Luce. I'll get them to bring the beds up and when I find the boxes with our bed linen, perhaps you can make them for me?' Lucy withdrew her finger from her mouth. 'Okay Mum. I can do that.'

'Good girl,' she said, hugging her briefly before running back downstairs to provide a few directions to the men. Although Dave was quite rotund, he was strong and she was pleased to see he was lifting as much as Jimbo, even if he didn't move as quickly. Nik dashed out of the house, intending to jump into the back of the truck to find the bedlinen boxes, when she walked straight into the back of Robbie. He was walking backwards with her dining table, a large solid timber piece she knew was heavy. At the other end of the table was a younger version of Robbie. Tall, good looking, dressed in faded jeans, tee shirt, work boots, and a big grin. They lowered the table to the ground for a moment.

'Nicola. This is my boy Harry. Harry, Mrs Reid.'

Wiping his hand on his jeans, Harry stepped forward. 'Nice to meetcha Mrs Reid.' He was young, late teens maybe. Nik shook his hand firmly. 'Please, call me Nik. Nice to meet you too.' Turning to Robbie she added, 'I looked for you to say thank you. I didn't expect you to come back and help with this.' She waved toward the truck. 'Happy you did though, we had no chance of getting it all off before dark without you. I'm not sure how I can thank you for your help today. Umm, I can pay you, and Harry, of course.'

Robbie looked at her for a moment. He spoke slowly, quietly.

'We're neighbours. It's what we do out here. I'm sure there'll be occasions when we help each other out. Don't give it another thought. Now, tell me where this goes.' As he finished, his smile broadened, and his eyes crinkled a bit. She wasn't sure how old he was, mid-forties maybe with a grown son, but she instinctively liked him.

'You may regret choosing to bring this monster in. It goes upstairs.' She grinned back at him.

Picking up the table, he nodded at Harry. 'You right at your end son?'

'Good as gold Dad.'

Turning to Nik, he said 'Lead the way Nicola. Or can I call you Nik too?'

Running up the stairs in front of them, she called down. 'Nik. Please. All my friends call me Nik.'

SHE WIPED HER BROW AS THE TRUCK DROVE AWAY. IN THE END, Dave hadn't charged anything extra, as Robbie and Harry had provided free labour.

'I can't thank you enough. I mean it. For cutting up the tree, then unloading the truck.' Although exhausted herself, she knew she should offer something for their trouble. 'I don't have any cold beer, but there are a couple of bottles of coke in the esky, if you'd like a drink. And I can make some ham and cheese toasted sandwiches …'

Putting his hat on, Robbie patted her shoulder gently. 'We're fine thanks Nik. We've got steaks to throw on the barbie at home. And cold beer. You must be exhausted. You've worked as hard as any of us today. Make those toasted sandwiches and wash them down with a coke.' She nodded gratefully. 'And you might want to fix something for the little ghost who has been busy upstairs all afternoon. It seems she has made the beds for you and set up your bookshelves.'

She looked at him, surprised. Lucy had been almost invisible, disappearing when she heard anyone coming upstairs. 'My daughter Lucy. She's very shy.' A movement at the top of the stairs told her Lucy was hovering just out of sight, listening.

Slightly louder, Robbie added, 'Lucy is a good little worker then. You'll be as pleased as punch when you see how much she's achieved.' A muffled giggle from upstairs warmed her heart. Quietly, she looked at both men, Harry standing as tall as his father. 'Thank you for today. For everything.'

'No worries Nik. We'll see you soon.'

'Bye Nik.' This from Harry.

Dragging her tired feet up the stairs, Nik found Lucy's arms around her waist, her lovely face looking up at her. Holding her tightly, Nik brushed the long brown hair from her forehead before leaning down to place a kiss on the tip of her nose. 'Was it okay for you today Luce? You didn't mind so many people here?'

'No. I was a bit scared at first. I don't think the men from the truck saw me at all, but the cowboys did. They pretended they didn't. After a while I wasn't frightened of them at all.'

Ruffling her daughter's hair, Nik took a deep breath. 'You know what? I don't think any of them were scary. Or bad. And I think you were very brave to help as much as you did.' Taking her hand, they walked to the kitchen. 'Would you like a toasted sandwich? And a drink? I see you have the beds made and found our towels and bathroom things. How about something to eat and drink, then a quick shower and straight to bed for us. What do you say?'

'Yes please Mum. It's been a big day. But I think I'm going to like it here.'

'I hope so, Luce. I've got a feeling this is the right place for us.'

2

Waking in a pool of sweat, pre-dawn light creeping through the bedroom window, Nik sat up quickly, her heart racing. Faint sounds came from inside the house. Unsure if it was just the normal creaking of the old building or if someone was moving around, she glanced at the other side of her bed. Lucy had slept with her last night, not keen to spend the first night in her own room. The bed was empty.

Probably Lucy then. She sat on the edge of the bed for a moment, hand on her heart, willing it to slow down. Taking two deep breaths, she called out. 'Luce. Is that you?'

Silence for a moment. 'Yup. It's me. Stay there, Mum, I'll be right in.'

Moments later Lucy appeared at the bedroom door, carrying a mug of steaming tea. Grinning, she walked carefully to the bedside table, placing the mug down. 'Thought I'd surprise you. Good morning, Mum.'

'Thank you, sweetheart, good morning to you too. What a lovely thought. Have you been awake long?'

'About an hour. I slept really well, but when you started to get restless, I got up and left you to sleep. You worked really hard yesterday.'

Sliding back on the bed, Nik rested her shoulders against the wall and took a sip of her tea. She'd kill for a coffee. Barista made. But this was nice. And Lucy having the confidence to move around the house while she slept. That was extra nice. A really good sign. She rolled her head from side to side, releasing the tension in her neck.

'Yup. I'm sore in all sorts of places. Especially my legs. Carrying stuff up and down the stairs will have done that. A quick breakfast and then we can unpack the rest of our stuff up here, get this area feeling like home.' Reaching out to Lucy, now sitting on the edge of the bed, she opened her arms. Lucy fell into them, half laying across Nik's lap, her head burrowed into her shoulder.

'What do you think so far?'

Sitting up, looking into her mother's eyes, Lucy reached out and tucked Nik's hair behind her left ear, gently sweeping it back from her forehead. She traced the jagged scar, beginning to fade, that ran from Nik's forehead, almost in her hairline, to her ear.

'Does it bother you Mum? The scar?'

While not surprised by the change of subject, Nik hesitated for a moment. 'No, the scar doesn't bother me. I don't care about this scar, or any of the others. I'm simply happy we're together. And safe.'

'I'm always safe with you Mum.' A tear trickled down Lucy's

face. 'I'm sorry he hurt you. I'm sorry I couldn't stop him. I tried.'

Pulling her daughter into her arms, Nik gulped, trying not to cry. 'It's not your fault. None of it was your fault.'

'It wasn't your fault either, Mum.' They held each other tightly, memories flooding Nik's mind as she drew a sharp breath. They had to stop reliving it. They had to start living beyond it. Months of counselling and Lucy could at least speak of it, but Nik worried it would always be her first thought on waking each day. They both needed to move past that. She kissed Lucy's forehead, and gently moved her to the side, reaching for her mug of tea.

'Well?'

'Well what, Mum?'

'What do you think? Of the place? Have you had a bit of a look around?'

Lucy smiled, stood, and walked to the window overlooking the paddock beside the house, the ragged mountain ranges of the State Forest and National Park rising steeply beyond. The distant peaks were tinged with blue, a trick of Australian euca-lypts. The heavily forested hills flowed down from the mountain peaks to rich green farmland below. Patches of black and bare spots were a roadmap to the destructive fires that had burned through thousands of hectares the previous summer.

'Yes, I like it. It's peaceful, but sort of wild at the same time. There was a kookaburra just outside the kitchen window earlier. It made me laugh. And I love that we're going to plan the reno-vations together, and even do some of the work ourselves. It will be like episodes of The Block.'

Warmed by the enthusiasm in Lucy's voice, Nik stood and stretched, swallowing the last of her tea. 'I'm going to throw some shorts and a tee shirt on, like you. It's going to be hot again today. Can you get some toast started? Or would you prefer eggs?'

'Toast is good. I turned the fridge on earlier and moved everything from the esky into it.'

'Good thinking. You start the toast; I'll be there in a moment.' Nik padded to the bathroom down the hall as Lucy returned to the kitchen.

Brushing her teeth, then washing her face, Nik looked at herself in the old, discoloured mirror. Taking a deep breath, she pulled her thick shoulder-length hair into a ponytail. It made her look younger than her thirty-eight years, but the scar in her hairline was visible. Other scars, one across her ribs and another on her shoulder were rarely seen. Throwing on a sleeveless tee and yoga shorts, she glanced at the back of her legs. A faded welt was visible where her shorts ended. Shrugging, Nik glanced in the mirror again. Wide-set eyes stared back at her with a few small lines creasing their corners when she smiled. Her lips were plump and naturally red, her nose was straight and her brows dark and arched. She touched her cheeks, thankful her skin was lightly tanned, with a few freckles across the bridge of her nose.

A faint smell of mould permeated the room. She wrinkled her nose. Maybe they could re-do this bathroom when they did the downstairs one. It would certainly be more comfortable.

The kitchen was large, with timber cabinets and benchtops most likely put in during the eighties and the old electric stove had seen better days. There was no dishwasher, but a large cement sink crouched beneath a large window, which Lucy had opened, letting in fresh air and a light breeze.

Lucy was standing at the toaster humming quietly to herself, two plates already piled with thick toast. Nik paused in the doorway. Her sweet daughter at eleven was long-limbed and coltish, her arms and legs lanky and thin. Wearing denim shorts and a pale green tee shirt, her thick, long dark hair was pulled up into a high ponytail, complete with multicoloured scrunchie. That was a good sign too. For months she had preferred to keep her hair down, hiding behind it when anyone spoke to her.

Lucy turned, waving a piece of toast in her hand, a small smear of vegemite on the side of her mouth. 'Started without you,' she giggled and raised an eyebrow, her face a girlish twin to Nik's.

'Good. I'll have butter and vegemite too, thank you.' Turning around in a circle Nik gestured to the room. 'It's a good size, don't you think? Perhaps we don't need to do much here. We could paint the timber cupboards and laminate the benchtop, put in a new stove, preferably gas. There's plenty of bench space and I really love the old sink, it might be the original.'

'I love that idea!' Lucy's eyes were shining.

'We could get it done soon, too, if we don't have to replace the cupboards. We could do most of this ourselves.' Nik waved her arm at the cupboards as she turned around.

'Okay, we'll look at paint colours for the cupboards online, I'll get my iPad.' Nik walked back to the bedroom, grabbed her iPad from her tote bag and sat it on the kitchen bench. They scrolled through several ideas on Pinterest, eating their breakfast standing at the bench. A few ideas seemed good, but they needed to get to a hardware store for paint samples.

Breakfast finished; they placed their plates into the large sink. 'I know the drought has broken but let's not fill the sink until we have lunch dishes too. It will save water.'

Lucy laughed. 'We might need a dishwasher Mum. You hate

washing up in the sink. Using the drought as an excuse is kinda funny.'

Nik poked her tongue out. 'We're on tank water out here, I need to check the tanks are full. The solicitor handling the sale made enquiries with Council. If we start offering short term accommodation we may be required to put in more tanks.'

Continuing to laugh, Lucy said, 'Yeah, I totally get that. But Mum, you really do hate washing up.'

Laughing together, Nik gave in. 'You're right. We need to make room for a dishwasher.'

SORTING THROUGH THE KEYS THE REAL ESTATE AGENT HAD provided, they strolled around the side of the house to the cottage. Originally stables, the lower walls were built from hand-made bricks, then timber boards above that. The paint was peeling on the outside at the front, but a veranda had been added on each side, with doors opening onto it. They were the original stable doors, with a top and bottom half. Nik and Lucy looked at each other, hand over mouths, exclaiming in unison. 'I love these doors, they're perfect!' Nik added, 'they need sanding and repainting, or we could even take them back to the original timber because I suspect they are Australian cedar under all those layers of paint.'

Lucy nodded and took her mother's hand, leading her around to the front of the building. The front door was a wide, modern double door. Nik unlocked it and they walked in, looking back at the entrance. 'Hmmm. Cheaply made and doesn't fit with the look of the building. Those doors have to go.'

'Hey Mum, do you think the entrance originally had a big

sliding stable door, or perhaps heavy timber double doors? Because I think that would look awesome.'

Nik glanced at her daughter's excited face, then walked back to the entrance, studying the opening a bit closer. 'It may have had no doors, just been an opening big enough to get a horse and wagon through. But there's no reason we can't get a door made that fits the style. Like a big sliding stable door.' Turning she winked at Lucy. 'You have great ideas.'

The inside was an open living area with a kitchenette at the far end and bedrooms on one side. Dated carpet covered the floor, plus the building needed painting inside and out and the kitchenette was just a small sink, aged cooktop, and a free-standing cupboard. 'We can pull this out ourselves and replace it with a neat little prefab kitchenette in a heritage style.' Nik took Lucy's hand, walking toward the bedrooms.

Two enormous bedrooms with a bathroom between them opened up to the veranda, taking up the whole length of the building on one side. They were completely bare of cupboards or furnishings. Lucy frowned. 'Would we put in wardrobes Mum? The rooms seem really empty.'

'People don't always unpack, but I think we could do a chest of drawers and maybe some hanging space. Folks don't need a lot for short term stays.' She walked into the bathroom, which had a door leading into it from each bedroom. It was a dark, narrow space, with just a basin, shower, and toilet. No frills. It all needed to be replaced. Nik stepped into the next bedroom, then back through the bathroom.

'The bedrooms are huge, and the bathroom basic and narrow. What if we took another metre from the side of each bedroom to add to the bathroom? That would give us about three point five metres by four metres. We could set it up really nicely with a large double shower, put the toilet in its own little room at one end and put a big claw foot tub on the veranda end, maybe add in a window there for extra light and ventilation.'

'I love it! It will be luxurious on the inside, but rustic on the outside. I can't wait to get started. Will we get this ready first, or the bit underneath the house?' Lucy was almost dancing on the spot with enthusiasm.

'I planned to do the house bit first but seeing this now, makes me believe we could get this cottage started straight away. We can finish by Easter and have guests staying, although probably just on weekends, and that will help us kick on with the house. It would be nice to get our own kitchen and bathroom done sooner, rather than later. I need to make a budget and we can schedule the work in stages. I have enough left from the sale of our old house to do the cottage, at least.'

They walked back toward the main house. The driveway stretched before them, deep potholes in the ground, long grass to the sides and many of the trees still reaching out across the road haphazardly. 'We need to get these trees cut back, just a little, and the driveway graded, and some gravel added. The recent rains have made it really rough and people coming from the city won't be keen to drive their cars in here, like this.'

'Do you think the cowboys could cut the trees back? Cowboy Dad has a chainsaw.' Lucy looked up at her mother.

'Maybe. I didn't get his number yesterday, but his name is Robbie Stewart. I can google, see if I can find him. He may be able to quote.' Nik pulled her phone from her back pocket. 'He might recommend local builders and tradespeople too. I was going to get recommendations from Ben Evans, the real estate agent, but I doubt he'll open again until Tuesday.'

Nik couldn't find anything under Robbie Stewart, or Robert

Stewart. She tried R. Stewart. Up popped a listing *R & J Stewart, Builders. No job too big or too small. Carpentry, fencing, tree lopping.* He had a mobile number. Nik looked at her watch. It was nine o'clock, but Sunday morning. Her finger hovered over the call button.

'I could just ask if he is interested in the tree lopping, giving a quote. It doesn't have to be today.' Lucy nodded, her face bright and excited. Nik pushed the button.

It rang a few times, then went to voicemail. A recorded woman's voice came on: *You've called R and J Stewart, builders. Please leave a message and we will return your call as soon as possible.*

'Um, hello, um Robbie. And Harry. It's Nicola Reid, your new neighbour. Can you give me a call back on this number when you have a moment please?'

3

_____

They hadn't heard the vehicle, but a car door slamming, and a man's voice brought a look of terror to Lucy's face. Nik glanced at her, saying calmly, 'Just stay up here, Luce, I'll go down and check who it is.'

Lucy nodded but stayed where she was, sitting on her bed. They had been sorting out her clothes and books and putting them away. There hadn't been much cupboard space in her bedroom, so together they had half dragged, half pushed a chest of drawers from Nik's room. They had cleaned a bit too and Nik was hot and sweaty and pulled at a piece of cobweb that had found its way into her hair as she ran down the stairs, two at a time.

Opening the front door, she saw a large Landcruiser ute, with a black and white border collie tied in the back, its tongue lolling in the heat. 'Hi Nik!' Robbie Stewart walked from the side of the house, a tin doggie bowl full of water in his hand. He placed it down in the shade of the veranda, then spoke as he untied the dog. 'Hope you don't mind, but Scout has been in the back of the ute on the way back from town, and she could do with a drink.'

'Hi Robbie. No, I don't mind at all.' She stood back as he let the dog jump down, the lead rope in his hand. Scout walked over to the bowl and began to lap thirstily. He dropped the lead on the ground, gave the dog a pat, and said 'Stay.' Scout immediately sat on her haunches, her tail swishing the veranda boards, her mouth half-open in a happy doggie smile.

'I got your message this morning, Nik, but had to finish a small job off in town. Thought I'd drop by on my way home. Is there something I can help you with?' He glanced at her shorts, and Nik suddenly felt exposed, tried to give her shorts a surreptitious tug. There was something about the way he looked at her.

'We've been unpacking. It's a hot day.'

He smiled, folded his arms, and leant back against the veranda post. 'I can see that.'

'I didn't get your number yesterday, but I googled you. I'm needing quotes for a few things and initially thought you might be able to recommend builders and tradespeople, but I see you're a builder yourself. I'm not sure what your workload is like, but are you interested in doing some work here?'

'We've got a few jobs on the go, and one big one up at Rawdon Vale, but Harry is staying up there this week to finish that off. Tell me what you need, I can work out some costs and timing for you.'

Relieved to be talking business, Nik said, 'I'll just nip in and get my iPad. We made a list of priorities this morning.'

Running back up the stairs, she saw Lucy hovering. 'It's Robbie, from yesterday. He's going to give me some quotes.'

'Cowboy Dad?'

'Yes. The son is called Harry, but he's somewhere else this week.'

'Okay.'

Back outside, Nik pulled her list up on the iPad.

'The driveway is my most immediate concern. Are you able to lop some of the trees back a bit? I could use the wood for fire-wood in the winter.'

'Sure. They don't need much. You won't often have such large vehicles coming in like yesterday. Some of the branches are overhanging too much. I would just cut those back. They make quite a nice avenue in the entrance. Better to cut them back every year or two, than to go hard and lose the aesthetic appeal of the driveway.'

'Yes. Good. Right. I'll need a price for that. And do you know anyone who could grade and gravel the driveway? The rain has made big pot-holes and some folk in city cars might find it tricky to navigate.' Noting his raised eyebrows, she added, 'I'm going to offer short term accommodation.'

Taking his hat off, he ran his hand though his thick chestnut hair, walking back to the worst of the holes in the driveway. 'Grading and adding crushed metal, then rolling it to compact it a bit would be best. But if we get heavy rain it will wash out again.' He strode further up the driveway, then walked into the long grass beneath the trees on each side. 'I recommend we dig a small drainage channel close to the trees, direct the water flow away from the road and back into the paddocks on either side. That will help the driveway last longer.'

Nik had followed him, not sure what he was thinking as he walked under the trees, even peering over the fence into the paddocks beside the driveway. She couldn't help but notice his long legs, clad in the same faded jeans as yesterday. Broad shoulders, tall, lean through the middle. Not a heavy drinker then.

'The paddock on this side of the fence is mine, so that's okay, but the other side is my neighbours, and I would need permission to redirect rain run-off in there.'

Robbie beckoned her forward, walking to the fence of the neighbouring property. The trees were on her side of the fence. Robbie had one elbow up on a fence post. 'There is an old bathtub in there, it's a water trough for cattle in this paddock. The trough is slightly downhill, we could capture the run-off in a small tank in the ground here, then gravity feed the water run-off to the trough, using a poly pipe. It's a little more to set up but will mean you won't need to keep grading and gravelling the driveway after heavy rain.'

'It sounds sensible Robbie, but I still need to talk to the neighbour. Do you know who owns this piece?'

Robbie turned to her, grinning, then jammed his hat back on his head. 'I do, Nik. My place starts here at this paddock, then runs along the road apiece, some of it running up into those hills there.'

She looked where he pointed. Surprised, but pleased, too. 'I understood all the forest area was owned by the State?'

'Not all, a lot of it on this side of the hill is privately owned. Over the hill it gets steep. That's all State Forest. And further up the road toward The Tops, it's National Park.'

They began to walk back toward the house. Nik caught a flash of colour on the second-floor veranda. Lucy was sitting in the shade, watching.

'Did you know the previous owners? Why did you never work out a deal to fix the drainage on the driveway with them?'

Nik knew she sounded suspicious, but she wanted to make sure she was trusting the right person. She'd been wrong before.

'Yeah, you'd think. The last owner was elderly. When her husband was alive, he had his own grader blade on the front of a small tractor and used to keep the driveway neat himself. It was never a problem. But he died several years ago, she stopped having guests stay and it just got away from her. She had a stroke about a year ago. You bought it from her estate. Her kids live in the city, never come out here. They just wanted it sold.'

'Oh.' That made sense. All the buildings had an uncared for, unlived in feel. The agent said it had operated as a bed and breakfast until recently, but maybe that was more than a year or two ago.

Back at the main house, Nik reached down and gave Scout a pat. She rolled over on her back, her tummy rounded, the nipples visible. 'Is she …?'

'Pregnant. Yes. She'll whelp in about three weeks. She isn't doing any real work on the farm but loves coming with me in the ute. She's a fabulous working dog, has a lovely nature too.' He knelt, taking the dog's head in his hands, giving her a slow, luxurious pat. Nik's tummy flipped over. He was so gentle. Such big, gentle hands. She stepped away. Seeing such gentleness in a man, after the violence she had experienced, sent her heart racing.

'Can I offer you a drink, Robbie. Coke? Water?'

'No thanks, Nik. I'll work out a price for the driveway grading, crushed gravel, and the tree lopping. I have a grader tractor myself, so I can do it all, no need for another contractor. I'm not going to charge for the drainage and poly pipe, as I will get the benefit of the extra water in this paddock for stock. It'll allow me to run a few more heifers here.' He pulled out his phone and tapped a few figures into his calculator. Looking up, he named a price. Much less than Nik had expected.

'Really? Oh, that's good. Thank you.' Nik watched Robbie untie the dog, tip the remaining water out of the bowl, then open the tray of the ute for her to jump up. 'When do you think you could start on it?'

'I'll come back after lunch to get the trees sorted today, grade tomorrow morning, bring a load of gravel in the afternoon, then roll it on Tuesday. If we get a few showers later in the week, I'll roll it again then. We aren't expecting heavy rains just yet, but when Harry returns next week, we can dig the drain and set up the water diversion.' He stepped forward, holding his hand out. Nik shook it.

'Do you want this in writing, Nik? I can send it through tonight.'

'That would be good. I need tax invoices, you know …'

'Sure. I'm not great with the bookwork, but I can do that.'

Robbie nodded, then walked swiftly around the side of his ute, jumped in, and pulled away. Leaning out he waved, looking up at the second floor.

Confused, Nik took a step back and looked up. Lucy was standing at the rail, in full view. Her hand still raised, waving as the vehicle made its way along the driveway to the road.

4

Lucy ran down the stairs as Nik stepped inside, the house several degrees cooler than outside.

'Did you see the dog, Mum? She's beautiful. All shiny and black and white and her tail kept wagging the whole time!'

Nik smiled and held her arms out. Lucy's face was radiant as she ran into them, quickly hugging her mother, then stepping back. 'What's her name? Did he tell you her name? I'm sure it's a her because I saw her nipple thingies.'

Laughing, she was delighted to see Lucy happy and chatty. Like she used to be. Before him. Before Nik's big mistake. 'Her name is Scout. You know, like the girl in *To Kill A Mockingbird.*'

'Scout.' Lucy said the name out loud, as if trying it on for size. 'Scout. I like that.'

'And she's going to have puppies in about three weeks, Robbie said.'

'Puppies? Really? How lovely.' Lucy was almost dancing on the spot. 'Is he going to do some work for us? Cowboy Dad?'

'Robbie. Mr Stewart to you; perhaps.' She laughed. Lucy's nickname suited the man. 'Yes, he is. He's going to come back after lunch and cut back the trees that are sticking out too far,' she pointed to the driveway, 'and then he will grade the driveway and add some crushed metal over the next couple of days. When his son, Harry, is back from another job later in the week they are going to dig a drain on that side,' Nik pointed to a dip in the grass, 'and send the rainwater into the paddock for his stock. He owns that piece and right up there to the mountains, so he's our neighbour. We're pretty lucky, he's going to do that drain bit for free, because he gets the water for his cattle.'

'That's good. Do you think he will bring Scout again?'

'I'm not sure Lucy, her puppies are due soon, so he said she isn't doing any farm work, just riding around to jobs with him in the ute.'

'Well, if he comes back in his ute, he might bring her. Do you think I could come down and pat her? You know, when he's working on the trees?' Lucy looked happy, and hopeful. It warmed Nik's heart. 'I was on the veranda. I let him see me. He saw me yesterday too, but he didn't say anything. Then I saw him put his hands on Scout. He has gentle hands. Someone who is gentle with a dog couldn't hurt a person, could they?'

'I don't think he would hurt anyone either, Lucy. And it's great you let him see you. Remember Doctor Slater said some people will just have a way about them that makes you feel safe. I think Robbie might be one of those people. If he brings Scout back, I'm sure you can pat her while he's working.'

They made lunch upstairs and ate their sandwiches while unpacking Lucy's room. It was looking good and would be even better when they painted and re-did the carpet. Or maybe pull the carpet up and polished the old floorboards. She'd have to see what condition they were in.

Nik hadn't asked Robbie to have a look at the cottage. She wanted to be sure his work was good first. She wondered what his wife was like, the woman on the voicemail message. She must be the J. in R and J Stewart.

Robbie came back after lunch, the back of his ute full of equipment, including a chainsaw. This time Scout was riding beside him on the passenger seat.

She walked out to greet him. 'I see you've brought Scout back. Lucy was quite taken with her earlier. You can leave her on the veranda again if you like.'

'Sure.' He smiled, his grey-blue eyes crinkling at the edges. His face was tanned, his teeth straight and white when he smiled. 'Scout's great with kids. I'll leave her bowl here, and perhaps Lucy can give her some water.'

Reaching into the back of the ute he lifted out his chainsaw, a small can of fuel and a pair of earmuffs. 'This may be noisy for a while. I'd recommend you do something inside while I get this bit done.'

Nodding, Nik watched him walk to the far end of the driveway with his gear. He was going to start there and work his way closer.

Lucy popped around the door, kneeling as she patted Scout, exclaiming at her softness. Scout gave her hand a couple of happy licks then laid her head in Lucy's lap, her tail pumping the veranda floor.

'Don't get too settled. Robbie asked if you could give Scout some water.' Nik handed the metal bowl to Lucy, who leaned close to the dog, explaining she would be back in a moment. She jumped up and ran to the tap at the side of the house under the water tank, filling the bowl and returning moments later, carrying it carefully.

'Would you like to make a jug of lemonade and some pikelets for afternoon tea?'

'We don't have any lemons.'

Taking Lucy by the shoulder, Nik turned her toward the water tank. 'See that tree just behind the tank? What does it look like to you?'

'Lemons! It's huge. Wow. I'll just get a basket from the kitchen.' Lucy shot off, returning with a wicker basket. 'I'll pick a dozen. Can I take Scout with me?'

Nik looked at Scout, who had sat up, looking eagerly at Lucy. 'Alright but take her on the lead and keep her close and in the shade. She's expecting puppies, remember.'

Nik checked her phone for the time, watching as Scout trotted happily at Lucy's side. She could probably do two hours of work while Lucy made afternoon tea and played with the dog. A room on the ground floor would be perfect for an office. It had an old solid timber countertop and may have been the reception desk for the police station at one time. She brought her laptop and work bag down and set it up, using a kitchen bar stool as a chair for the high counter. She had organised Wi-Fi connection before they arrived, so it didn't take long to get everything connected. This way she could offer free wi-fi to guests, too, when they eventually came.

In the meantime, she would continue to run her book-keeping practice from home. She had only retained a few long-term clients who could manage working with her remotely. It would be enough to keep them going and would help pay for any renovations that were beyond the money she had put aside.

Perhaps she'd even be able to pick up a couple of local clients. Robbie mentioned he didn't enjoy the paperwork side of his business, but maybe his wife did that for him. He said Scout would be alone at home, so it's possible his wife was away. Could be worth asking though.

Lucy returned and went upstairs to make afternoon tea, leaving Scout laying on the veranda. The noise of the chainsaw slowly grew louder, as Robbie worked his way closer to the house. After almost two hours it stopped altogether and Nik looked up, expecting to see him coming in for a cool drink. But he had gloves on and was working his way back up the driveway, stacking the sawn wood into piles as he went. Nik pulled on the gardening gloves Lucy had set aside after picking the lemons and strode down the driveway. She nodded at him, then began picking up some of the pieces, watching how he stacked them and following suit.

'This is heavy work for a woman and you're paying me to do it. You don't have to help.' It was quietly but firmly said.

'And I'm sure the cost of the drain is going to outweigh the financial benefit to you. So, I'll pick up a few logs and stack them.' Also said quietly, but firmly. He chuckled and kept working. She liked the sound.

At the end of the driveway, they stood for a moment, looking back towards the house. It was more visible now from the entrance, but Robbie had left enough foliage to create a welcoming avenue of green. Pulling her gloves off, Nik nudged Robbie with her shoulder. 'Nice work, Cowboy Dad.'

'Cowboy Dad?' he laughed loudly, a rich, hearty sound.

Nik chuckled. 'It's what Lucy calls you. Cowboy Dad. And Harry is Cowboy Son. She knows your names, but it's how she sees you.' Turning to him, she frowned slightly. 'I hope you're not offended. And she's made some lemonade from our own lemons and pikelets for afternoon tea. She's a great little baker.'

'Not at all. To a girl from the city, I must look like a cowboy. Pity I didn't ride a horse over to complete the look.' They began walking toward the house. 'A cold lemonade and pikelets sound perfect. I hope she lets me thank her.'

'Horse. You have a horse? Do you keep it nearby?' Nik looked across his paddocks, which seemed empty of stock.

'Horses. Plural. We have several. Harry rides in the camp draft and what we call 'sporting' at the local rodeos. Australian stock horses mostly. Quiet, good natured. Smart animals.'

'Oh. That's lovely.' Nik was deep in thought as they arrived at the house. Stepping inside she saw that Lucy had set a small table up in her office area, its surface neatly covered with a gingham cloth, a jug of lemonade, two glasses and a platter of pikelets with jam and cream positioned nicely in the middle.

Robbie hesitated in the doorway. 'I'll just nip around to the tap and wash my hands. Back in a moment.'

Nik went into the downstairs laundry to wash her hands and realised she was pleased to be sharing afternoon tea with him. Working alongside him had been good. Neighbourly. They arrived back together. Their first glass of lemonade went straight down, but they sipped on the second one. Robbie ate a pikelet, 'Delicious.' Nik knew Lucy would be listening at the top of the stairs.

Leaning back after his third pikelet, Robbie patted his flat stomach. 'Couldn't fit another thing in. Thank you, Nik. You must know a good bakery around here because I'm fairly sure the local one is closed today, and they are the best pikelets I've had in a long while.'

He was rewarded by a little giggle from the top of the stairs. Nik said, 'Wait until you taste her scones.'

Lucy called out from the top of the stairs. 'Lemon Meringue Pie!' Nik's surprise was evident, and Robbie looked pleased with himself. While he didn't know their story, he had surmised Lucy was shy with strangers.

Standing, Robbie nodded to the computer set up at the counter. 'Working?'

'Yes. I'm a bookkeeper. I had a practice in the city but sold it to make this move. I'm just keeping a handful of clients I've had for a long time, who don't mind working with me remotely.'

Robbie nodded. 'Good for you.'

She stood on the veranda while he reloaded his ute, putting Scout back in the passenger seat. He looked up and waved. 'Thank you for afternoon tea, Miss Lucy.'

Her girlish voice called down, 'My pleasure, Cowboy Dad.'

His eyes met Nik's as he looked across the bonnet of his ute at her. He smiled and nodded, and she grinned back, waving as he drove away.

Lucy flew down the stairs, giggling. 'He called me 'Miss Lucy' like a real cowboy would.'

'Yes, he did. And he is a real cowboy because he told me today, he, and Cowboy Son, have horses.'

'Ohhh! Horses! Maybe I can see them some time.'

'Sure. I'll check on that.'

5

The next few days flew by and Nik and Lucy focussed on setting things up inside the house while Robbie graded the driveway, delivered crushed gravel, then rolled it several times. Light overnight rain had created the perfect environment to get the job finished.

While she'd offered lunch each day, Robbie brought his own, including a small esky of cold drinks. He took his lunch break in the shade of the front veranda, where Scout lay as he worked. Nik often sat with him, but Lucy chose to stay inside, although she baked something for afternoon tea each day. Nik knew she heard his comments of appreciation for her efforts and was thrilled to see her lovely face glow with happiness at his words.

At times, while he was working at the far end of the driveway, Lucy would creep out to the veranda to sit with Scout, ensuring she had water in her bowl. The expectant dog's tail wagged madly when she appeared, and after a while she began to wriggle forward to lay her head in Lucy's lap.

By Friday morning Robbie had completed the driveway, coming to the front door later to advise Nik he would be taking his roller home, but could he leave the tractor around the back of the house, as he would use it with a different implement on the back to dig the drain down the side of the drive.

He leant against a veranda post, casually stroking Scout's head. Looking at her, his keen eyes taking in her appearance, he added, 'Harry will be home today, so we'll come back this afternoon with more equipment, and if it's okay with you we can get the drain finished over the weekend.'

Nik had pulled her hair back into a headband and knew her scar was visible. Somehow, she didn't mind him noticing and didn't feel she needed to provide an explanation. 'That's great. I'm thrilled with the driveway; it should hold up now even for the fussiest city driver.' She smiled broadly. 'Do you have an account for this work? I'm happy to pay it straight away.'

'Darn! I knew you'd ask me that. I'm not great with the bookwork. Harry will do the account for me later. We upgraded to Xero Accounting a few years ago, but I've never got the hang of it. Prefer to be doing the work than billing it.' He chuckled.

'You'd be surprised how many of my clients, especially tradespeople, feel the same.' Nik nodded as she spoke, but in the back of her mind wondered why his wife wouldn't be helping with the bookwork.

'Alright then, Nik. I'll head off. Will be back later today with Harry to drop the equipment off. We usually go into the pub on Friday night for a quiet ale and wood-fired pizza. Have you been into town at all?'

'I've nipped in a couple of times, picked up some sample paint pots from the hardware store. Most of the shops have been closed, but I did get a really good coffee from the place on the corner.'

'Oh, that's Debbie's place. Great business. Really good baked goods too, although you won't need that, you have your own baker on site.' He smiled warmly at her as he picked up Scout's almost-empty water bowl, tipping the last of the water onto the lavender growing to one side.

The warmth of his voice, the understanding implied, brought sudden tears to her eyes. She knew Lucy was hovering just inside, so she took a step forward. Reaching out, she touched his arm, speaking softly. 'Thank you. For all you've done this week.'

If he noticed the emotion in her voice, he didn't comment. He gave her a quick smile, slapping his hat on his head. 'All part of the service ma'am. See you later then.' Turning, he strode to his vehicle, his dog trotting beside him.

SITTING DOWN TO A LUNCH OF FRIED RICE MADE FROM LEFTOVERS; A favourite of Lucy's, Nik asked her how she was feeling about all they had achieved in their first week.

'I really love it here Mum. It's quiet and peaceful and I love it when Cowboy Dad brings Scout with him. She's so beautiful.' Lucy smiled shyly at her mum. 'Do you think we could get a dog one day? One like Scout?'

The thought had already crossed Nik's mind and she wondered if all Scout's puppies were spoken for. She didn't want to suggest it to Lucy in case they were. 'I think a dog is a lovely idea. You would need to look after it and train it if we got a puppy, or we could try the local pound and adopt a grown dog. Let's get some of this work done first, and then look into it.'

Lucy nodded happily as she took her plate to the sink. She had taken to plaiting her hair each morning and Nik could see she had gained confidence. While Lucy hadn't spoken directly to Robbie all week, she had waved at him from afar a few times and called out a greeting from the safety of the top balcony. Better than previous months when she wouldn't show herself to anyone at all. Nik had been home-schooling her for the last six months and was prepared to continue for a further year, at least. But now she wondered if Lucy would be okay to go to school. The nearest one, in Barrington Village, was small. They still had almost four weeks before first term began; perhaps she would be ready.

As they washed up together, they chatted about the cottage. 'I think we're ready to get some quotes for the cottage, Luce. We've got our part of the house clean and settled, and my office downstairs. I like the little sitting room you've created down there too. Robbie is a builder, how about we ask him to quote on the work? He would know plumbers and electricians too.'

'He's really nice Mum. I think it would be great if he could do the work on the cottage.' She drew in a breath. 'I'm going to talk to him soon. About his horses. Maybe not today, but soon.'

Nik put down the plate she was washing and hugged her daughter hard. 'That's brilliant, Luce. He's a kind man and I think he'd love to talk to you about his horses. When you're ready.'

THEY WERE IN THE COTTAGE WHEN ROBBIE RETURNED LATE IN THE afternoon, his ute full of black water pipe and other equipment. Harry drove in behind him in an older, battered ute. Nik walked from the cottage, wiping her hands on her cut-off jeans before raising one in a wave.

'Hi Nik.' Harry boomed out, already standing in the back of his vehicle, passing equipment down to his father.

'Do you need a hand?'

'Nah, almost got this lot unloaded. Did Dad tell you we're going to the pub for a cold one and some pizza? Welcome to join us if you like.'

'Oh, thanks Harry. Sounds delicious, but my daughter is a bit shy, so we don't go out to eat.'

Robbie walked around the back of the ute, giving his son a friendly pat on the shoulder as he jumped down from the tray back. He was dressed in dark jeans, dress boots and collared shirt, sleeves rolled to the elbows. What is it about him that set her hormones racing? She glanced at Harry again, also dressed in clean jeans and tee shirt. Drawing in a quick breath, Nik smiled to herself. The boys were in their going out gear. They scrubbed up okay.

'Can I ask you a favour, ladies?' Robbie glanced at Lucy, who was now standing in the shade of a large plum tree beside the house. Scout had jumped out of Robbie's car and was sitting at Lucy's feet.

Nik glanced at Lucy, pleased to see she was close enough to hear the conversation, and delighted to see her nodding and smiling shyly. 'Sure. How can we help?'

'We usually leave Scout tied in the back of the ute while we have a bite to eat at the pub. But she loves it here so much with Lucy, I wondered if we could leave her here for a bit and I'll pick her up around seven.'

'Yes please.' It was almost a whisper, but Nik heard it. Robbie looked directly at Lucy. 'Thank you, Lucy, I really appreciate that. By way of thanks, can I bring some pizza back for you? The pub does great takeaway.'

She glanced at her daughter. They both loved pizza, especially wood-fired, but lately they made their own at home. Lucy nodded eagerly. Nik laughed. 'That would be great. Thank you. We eat any pizza, but no anchovies or chilli.'

'Done. See you around seven.'

6

Nik cleaned up the downstairs sitting area while Lucy played on the lawn beneath the plum tree with Scout. The dog's water bowl, some doggy treats, and an old tennis ball had been left with her, and Lucy sat on the grass, throwing the ball a short distance. Scout ran to it eagerly, then trotted back, tail wagging and a doggy smile plastered on her face. After half an hour or so Nik noticed Lucy laying on the grass reading a book, Scout stretched out beside her in the shade. A lovely scene.

After doing some bookwork for a client, and answering a couple of emails, Nik went upstairs to have a shower. She washed her hair, leaving it to dry naturally into a wavy shoulder-length bob. She slipped on a sleeveless cotton dress, brightly coloured, that stopped short of her knees. Her legs were slim and tanned and she felt feminine for the first time since the move.

She set the table downstairs for dinner. They didn't need

much, a couple of plates, a jug of homemade lemonade and two glasses. She had planned to make a salad but knew Lucy would love just eating pizza from the box.

Scout pricked her ears as Robbie drove in, her tail thumping on the veranda. Lucy had been sitting beside her, but she stood and moved inside the house as Robbie got out, two pizza boxes in his hand.

'Hi Nik. Hope you're hungry, I've brought Margarita pizza and one with the lot, except anchovies and chilli.' He walked to the veranda and handed the boxes over, before bending down to pat Scout.

'Harry not with you?'

'Nah, he's catching up with mates. If he has a few beers he'll stay in town, come back here after breakfast to start on the drain job. Nineteen. I'm pretty lucky, he enjoys a few beers but doesn't overdo it, and he never drives if he's had a few.'

'What about you, Robbie. Do you enjoy a few beers? Or wine?' Nik asked, smiling, her eyebrows raised.

'I admit I used to hit it hard in my younger days, especially when I was on the camp draft circuit. But marriage and kids set me straight. Now I enjoy a couple of cold ones, may even crack the top off another one once I'm home, but that's it for me.' He glanced at her. 'What about you? Do you have a beer or glass of wine at the end of the day?'

'I used to. Wine mostly. Sometimes a beer. But lately, well, I need to be in the present, as the gurus say. Sometimes I yearn for a glass of wine. Especially after a busy, hot day. But it passes quickly.'

The aroma from the boxes was making her mouth water and Lucy hovered just inside the open door, waiting until Nik passed the pizzas to her. She looked at Robbie, saying almost apologetically, 'I'd ask you to join us …'

'Not at all. I've had my fill but thank you. Another time perhaps?' He whistled to Scout, who followed him to the car, jumping into the front when he opened the passenger door. He called, 'Thank you for looking after Scout, Miss Lucy. See you tomorrow.'

Lucy came to the door, not quite meeting his eye, her voice quiet. 'I love looking after Scout.' He waved to her and shot a grin at Nik, who beamed back at him. While he didn't know of their recent past, and the trauma they had suffered, she knew he sensed it. She felt herself warming to him and reminded herself he was married; she had noted the ring on his finger. She needed to establish a community here; friends, neighbours, people she could grow to trust. He hadn't mentioned his wife, but perhaps she was away. Nik hoped she was as welcoming as Robbie; it would be great to have adult female company here too.

THE BOYS WERE BACK ON THE JOB NEXT MORNING BY EIGHT O'CLOCK. If Harry had a big night, he certainly didn't seem any the worse for wear. In fact, she could hear him chatting to Robbie as they worked, and occasionally breaking into a song, something country, in a sweet, strong voice that carried. More than once she heard father and son joking and teasing one another. Nice people. Nice family. She would ask about his wife when they stopped for lunch. To raise a young man like Harry, she would be lovely, she was sure.

The drain seemed to have progressed well over the morning, and by noon the day was hot. Harry had taken his shirt off, his tanned torso rippling with muscle and the vigour of youth. They were tall, well-built men, Robbie broader at the shoulders, his biceps bulging as he worked with shovel and pickaxe while Harry operated the backhoe on the tractor.

Nik had a bucket filled with ice, several cans of coke, squash, and water chilling. Robbie looked back at the house, saw her standing there, one arm raised to shade her eyes. He looked at his watch, then called out to Harry, who stopped the tractor.

They walked toward the house, chatting. Harry grinning broadly. 'Put your shirt on son.' Nik heard Robbie's quiet words as they veered off to the side of the house to wash up at the tap from the water tank.

Faces washed, hair damp, they reappeared and sat on the veranda steps. 'Cold drink?' Nik gestured set the bucket near them.

Harry took a coke; Robbie grabbed a water. 'Thanks Nik,' they said in unison. Robbie pulled their own esky closer; he had left it in the shade of the veranda when they arrived. He passed a wrapped pack of sandwiches to Harry and an apple, pulling another out for himself. 'Sandwich, Nik?' he opened his pack, holding it out to her.

'Oh, thank you. No, we've got some salad ready for our lunch. Happy to share too, though.'

'All good. Sandwiches fill us up. The carbs are good for an afternoon working.'

Nik stepped inside, she had two bowls of salad on the downstairs table. Lucy was there. She silently handed a bowl, with fork, to Nik and nodded. Nik smiled and stepped back onto the veranda. 'We might join you if that's okay?'

'Sure.' Harry slid down to a lower step, Nik taking the spot Harry vacated, next to Robbie. Lucy dragged a chair from inside just to the doorway, eating her salad quietly. Scout got up from her place beside Robbie, sauntered over to Lucy and lay down at her feet.

Laughing, Harry looked directly at Lucy, then back to his father. 'Watch out Dad, Scout may have switched loyalties. It seems she's taken to Lucy.'

'That was obvious from the first day, son. Young Lucy has a way with animals, that's for sure.'

Nik turned around, curious to see if the men's comments would send Lucy back inside, but her cheeks were flushed, her head down. When she glanced up, she caught her mother's eye. Nik mouthed 'love you' to Lucy, who wrinkled her nose before going back to her salad.

To change the subject and take further pressure away from her daughter, Nik turned to Robbie. 'Your business, R and J Stewart. Is the J your wife Robbie? Is she away at the moment?'

Both men stopped eating. The silence stretched and Nik could see tension in Robbie's face. Jaw clenched; he drew in a deep breath. She glanced at Harry, who was looking at his father with … interest? Concern? Damn, she knew she had put her foot in it, but didn't know how to undo her words. About to speak again, apologise, change the subject, anything.

Robbie stood up, his voice low. 'Jessica, my wife, passed away three years ago. Planning to change the business name to R and H Stewart, now Harry's finished school and decided to work the business with me. Need to do that sooner, rather than later.' He picked up his esky, walking toward his ute. 'We'll get back to work now Harry, if you're done there.'

Placing the esky in the back of his ute, he stalked up the driveway toward the tractor. Scout whimpered and walked to Harry, who stood. He patted her head. 'It's okay, Scout. Stay here with Lucy.' He added with a sad smile, 'Mum had an aneurism. It was sudden. No warning at all. Dad … well, Dad struggles with it still. It's Mum on the voicemail message on the home phone, he won't change it.' He reached out, touching Nik's shoulder. 'There's no way you could have known. He'll burn some energy off working and will be fine in a while.'

As Harry walked away, she stood and moved quickly into the house, brushing past Lucy in her haste. Reaching her study, she sat and cried. The tears fell silently, she reached for a tissue and blew her nose. Small arms wrapped around her shoulders. 'It's okay, Mummy.' She hadn't called her Mummy since … before.

Nik wiped her eyes. 'I'm sorry Luce. I don't know what came over me. Why it affected me so much. Their story. Losing his wife, Harry his Mum. We didn't even know her.'

Lucy smiled wanly, before climbing into her mother's lap, putting her small hands on each side of her face, looking into her eyes. 'It's the love, Mum. The cowboys really loved her.' Sobbing again, Nik buried her head in Lucy's shoulders. She felt Lucy's tears too, her small sobs shaking her body.

Wetness on her arm made Nik jump. Scout was there, licking her arm, nuzzling Lucy's leg. They looked at each other, tears still falling, and began to smile, then laugh. Lucy slid off Nik's lap and threw her arms around the dog's neck while Nik slid to the floor with her, patting Scout with one hand, stroking Lucy's hair with the other. The noise of the tractor outside continued and she wasn't sure how long they sat there. Lucy looked up at her.

'You okay now, Mum?'

'Yes. I am. I really am. Perhaps a good cry is what I needed.'

She kissed the top of Lucy's head. 'How about you, sweetheart, are you okay?'

Lucy turned into her mother's body, hugging her tightly. 'Getting better every day.'

'I love you, Luce.'

'Love you too, Mummy.'

7

Nik was working at her desk when she heard the tractor stop. Looking at her watch, she saw it was almost five. A long day for the men in such hot weather. She stepped on to the veranda. Lucy and Scout were laying under the plum tree, Lucy reading aloud from a favourite book, the dog's head in her lap.

Robbie was doing something at the back of the tractor. Nik worried he was still upset, but she saw him look up at Harry, in the driver seat, and say something with a broad smile. Harry bantered back. Good. She wouldn't mention his wife again. They could get back to normal.

Harry started the tractor and waved to her as he turned it around and began driving away. Robbie strode toward her. 'You'll be pleased to know the noisy part is finished. Harry is taking the tractor home; I'll follow in his ute. Is it okay if mine stays here overnight?' He flashed her a relaxed smile and she smiled back. Good. The tension was gone.

'No problem at all, it's not in the way.'

'We'll be back tomorrow to finish running the poly pipe to the new tank, then to the water trough in the paddock. Should be hooked up and going by the end of the day.'

'You've done a great job. Really quick too.' They sat together on the veranda steps, Robbie accepting the bottle of cold water she handed him. 'I have plans for the cottage out back. Some renovations to update it for short term accommodation. Some of it needs a builder, but I also need a plumber and electrician. Are you interested in having a look tomorrow, listen to my ideas, and provide a quote? It would be great if you would project manage the other trades. I understand if you have other work on though now that the holidays are over.'

Turning to look at her, he spoke quietly. 'Harry's still working on the job up at Rawdon Vale. I'll have to go up there for a day mid-week to check on it, order more materials. We're building some new horse yards. The two boys from the farm up there are helping, they're a bit younger than Harry, but are working well and it's saving them some money.' He took a drink of water, his eyes on her as he did.

'I'd be keen to have a look at the cottage. I have a builder's licence, so there's no worries there. If you're not making changes to the footprint, extending, then you don't need to apply for Council approval.'

'No, not extending. All the changes are under roof. But I want to see if it's possible to move some internal walls, create a bigger bathroom space. Bathrooms and views seem to 'sell' holiday accommodation. I've certainly got the views, and proximity to National Park for walks and hiking.' Nik couldn't keep her excitement for the project from her voice.

Robbie was smiling and grinning. It seemed to Nik her

enthusiasm was contagious. 'I work with all the local trades, I'll have a walk through with you tomorrow, then get back to you with some quotes. You mentioned paint samples the other day, are they for the cottage, or the house?'

'Both!' Nik giggled. 'Lucy and I got a bit carried away with our ideas. There are little splotches of paint all over the place. It will be hard to choose. But the cottage first, to get some paying customers, while we do up the downstairs part of the house. If possible, we'll make some changes to the kitchen upstairs, we need a bigger commercial style oven, plus upgrades in the bathroom. I was thinking of putting in an ensuite too, but really, with extra bathrooms down here it's probably not needed.'

'Okay. Cottage first then.' He stood, looking down at her, still smiling. 'Well, I'll be off, back again tomorrow.'

'Thanks again. You and Harry are quite the team. Can't believe how much you got done today.' Nodding happily, he got into Harry's ute, settling the dog beside him before driving away.

If he looked in his rear-view mirror as he drove slowly out, he would see Lucy step on to the veranda, to wrap her arms around her mother's waist.

TOSSING AND TURNING THAT NIGHT, THE SHEETS TWISTED AROUND her legs, her hair damp, Nik finally got up and sat in a chair by her bedroom window. The window faced the ragged mountain ranges, the moon providing enough light to see the steep hills climbing skyward. Robbie's home was out that way. She could see lights twinkling in the distance. Drawing her knees up, she rested her chin on them, staring pensively out the window.

Hot and sweaty, the vivid dream had awakened her from a deep sleep. Not the recurring nightmare she had been struggling with for six months. This dream had been slow, gentle. She had been laying under the plum tree in the soft grass, Robbie's dog, Scout, sprawled nearby. A man had appeared, she couldn't see his face at first, but knew it was Robbie. He lay beside her, on one elbow, tracing the scar on her face with tender hands. He kissed the scar, as she smiled through soft tears. His lips moved across her face, to her mouth. Kissing gently, he nibbled her bottom lip. She shook her head, smiling and crying all at once. He kissed her eyes, kissed her tears away. Then moved slowly down to her mouth. Shaking her head, she kept her lips closed but he persisted, gently, looking into her eyes. Tingling, she closed her eyes and opened her lips. As he took her mouth with his, heat rose from her body. Her arms came up around his neck, tugging him closer. He kept kissing her, running one hand down her side, tentatively touching her breast, before moving lower. Her thighs were bare, she was wearing the bright cotton frock. He moved his hand upwards, along her thigh to her hip, then across to the centre of the heat that pulsed within her. And she woke.

This was no good. She couldn't have romantic thoughts about her neighbour. About anyone for that matter. She had to think of Lucy. She would always come first. She would never make that mistake again. No matter how genuine, or caring the man seemed to be. She couldn't, wouldn't, take the risk.

By morning she had set the dream, and the feelings it engendered, aside. Robbie would be a friend. A good friend. He was still in love with his dead wife. He hadn't shown any interest, hadn't made any suggestions, or even looked at her in a way that might indicate interest. It was just her fevered, hormonal body that had betrayed her in the dream. She would remain friendly, build a community around her as she planned. Friends, neighbours, townsfolk. She would build a life here for her and Lucy. A life that would keep them safe. Keep Lucy safe. Help her heal. They would never forget, but they could heal and move past it.

8

Nik had finally returned to sleep in the early hours of the morning, only to wake with Lucy shaking her shoulder and the sun shining brightly through the window. 'Mum, Mum! Cowboy Dad's back. He has a horse Mum. Hurry, you need to see this!'

Jumping up, Nik pulled on denim shorts, bra, and tee shirt. Lucy hovered while she brushed her teeth, then ran downstairs together. Scout was sitting on the veranda, her tail thumping against the floorboards when she saw them. Lucy grabbed Nik's hand, pulling her down the steps, heading toward the fence of Robbie's paddock.

Sure enough, there he was with a chestnut horse, still saddled, out by the water trough. Lucy waved and called out, 'Cowboy Dad!'

He grinned, then walked over to the fence, leading the horse behind him. 'This is Honey, I'm going to leave her and another horse in this paddock now that I have the water trough working. Thought I'd ride her over.'

Lucy stepped forward. Nik was amazed. 'Oh, she's beautiful. Can I pat her?'

'Of course. Let me help you over the fence.' He held the wires apart as Lucy slipped through, her shyness dissolving in her excitement.

'Honey is a mare and is carrying a foal, she isn't due for another six months so I'm still riding her. She's quiet, but you must always speak to her as you walk towards her, so she knows you're there. Never come up behind her quietly, as she might get a fright and kick, or take off. Come close to me, you can pat her neck, like this.' Robbie demonstrated. Lucy, eyes shining, imitated all he did, listening carefully as he explained some basic horse lore.

Nik was speechless as she watched Lucy act without shyness around Robbie. Her daughter's confidence grew as he walked her around the horse. Climbing through the fence, Nik approached the mare, petting her gently on the side of her face, before scratching under her chin and smiling as Honey nuzzled her.

'Would you like to sit on her Lucy, while I lead you around?' Robbie smiled gently and Lucy nodded and grinned. 'Yes please.' Not a whisper this time.

Holding Honey's bridle, Robbie explained how to mount using the stirrup. Lucy wasn't quite tall enough to get her foot in the stirrup, so Robbie told her to put her left foot in his linked hands, then to swing her right leg over and settle into the saddle. Once mounted she laughed happily. 'Mum, look at me. I'm riding Honey!'

Nodding, Nik grinned back, while Robbie took the reins and

walked the horse, with Lucy holding the front of the saddle, across to the water trough, around it, then back to Nik. Just then, Harry's ute idled up the driveway.

'Harry's here. I'll unsaddle Honey now. We need to finish the last bit of the drainage and check it's all working. Then I'm going to have a look at what you and your Mum want to do with the cottage.' He spoke directly to Lucy. She nodded.

'Do you know how to dismount? Left foot in the stirrup, then swing your right leg over. You might have to make a little jump at the end.' Holding Honey's head, he looked up at her. 'Want to give it a try yourself?'

Lucy nodded. 'Yes, thank you.' She managed to get off without incident, receiving a quick grin from Robbie. 'Well done, you're a natural.' Turning to Nik he raised an eyebrow. 'Would you mind if I left her tack here, Nik. On the side veranda perhaps? Harry's brought a box of kit with him, her brushes and spare halter.'

Lucy was nodding wildly at Nik, her eyes shining. 'Of course. But perhaps better to put it in the laundry, there's plenty of room. I'd hate possums to chew the leather if we left it out.'

'Thank you, that's perfect.' He unsaddled the horse, explaining everything to Lucy as he went.

Harry appeared at the fence beside Nik. 'She's a lovely mare. Nice and quiet. Dad has two more he'll move into this paddock to keep her company. I've brought a bale of hay too, although the feed in here is quite good.' He called out to Lucy, holding a brush in his hand. 'I have Honey's brush here, Lucy, if you'd like to use it. Always good to brush her after the saddle comes off.'

Eyes wide, Lucy looked at Harry. He was holding the brush out over the fence. She hesitated, looked down at her feet, then at Nik. She recognised the sudden look of fear in Lucy's eyes and was about to intervene, not wanting to spoil the moment for her daughter, who had taken such big steps already, in just a few days.

Lucy looked up, directly at Harry. She gave him a tentative smile, then walked over to the fence and took the brush from his hand, turning quickly and walking back to the horse. She reached up to stroke the brush down Honey's shoulder, then looked back. 'Thank you.' It was said quietly, but Nik and Harry heard it.

'Right then, Nik. Show me where I can put the bale of hay and I'll get it unloaded while Dad brings the saddle and bridle back to the house.' Harry held the fence wires for Nik to step through, giving her a friendly pat on the shoulder as they walked back to his ute.

Glancing over her shoulder, Nik saw Lucy walking back with Robbie. He had the saddle over one arm, while she held the bridle. He was speaking to her as they walked and she was looking up at him, nodding every now and again. Taking a deep breath, Nik directed Harry to leave the hay bale outside the laundry door. Robbie stepped up on the veranda, then through to the laundry as she held the door open. There was an old wooden chest against one wall. 'Right there would be good, and there's a hook on the wall you can hang the bridle on, if you like.'

'Right-oh, that's perfect. I hope it won't be in your way.'

Lucy handed the bridle to Robbie, who hung it on the hook. 'Well done, Miss Lucy. You're going to be a fine horsewoman.' She giggled, leaning into Nik's side.

'I think you're right Robbie.' Nik ruffled her daughter's hair.

∼

HARRY LEFT AFTER LUNCH. THEY HAD ALL SAT ON THE VERANDA, sharing sandwiches and the scones Lucy had baked during the morning. Robbie stood, picked up his hat and turned to them. He had a small notepad in his top pocket and a pen, which he pulled out. 'Let's go and inspect the cottage, see what you want to do over there.'

Nik stood and looked at Lucy. Do you want to come too, Luce?'

'No thanks, Mum. I'll take the glasses and plates in, then I'll play under the tree with Scout for a bit.'

Walking across to the cottage, they didn't speak. As she opened the front door, Nik turned to see Lucy taking their lunch things into the house.

'I want to thank you, Robbie, for all you've done this week. With Lucy. Bringing Scout and now Honey. This is the happiest she has been, in a long time.' Nik wanted to tell him more, felt she should explain, but her eyes filled with tears. The morning had been beautiful. Watching Lucy so animated, and fearless.

He closed the door behind them and turned to her. He reached out and took her in his arms, holding her against his chest while she sobbed. 'I don't know what you've been through, Nik. You and Lucy. But I can see it was traumatic. For you both. Lucy reminds me of a young horse; skittish, shy, and fearful. She needs to learn to trust again, to feel safe. Being around animals, dogs and horses, will help.' Nodding into his chest, Nik's sobs subsided.

Nik took a step back, slightly embarrassed. Robbie gave off an air of quiet understanding.

'You're right. I was letting her hide away. I haven't wanted to force Lucy to face her fears, instead I was hoping the fresh start would eventually do that for her. We need friends here, like you and Harry. Thank you.'

Robbie smiled and looked down at her. 'We are friends. And neighbours. We're going to be living side by side for a long time. We're off to a good start.'

'Now, about this cottage.' He pointed to the front doors. 'I hope you're going to tell me those cheap and ugly doors have to go!'

She threw her head back and laughed. 'Yes. First thing to go. Absolutely. Lucy wondered if we could do a big sliding stable door instead, something in solid timber.'

Glancing at her, Robbie grinned and walked back to the doors, pulling out a tape measure as he went. 'Yep. That would work.' He looked around the big living area, a frown on his face. 'You know, I recall a big set of double doors here before. Solid rosewood. They'd been painted over a few times and I'm not sure why they replaced them. Probably for a nineteen-eighties style upgrade.' He snorted. 'But I wonder if they are still here, stored in one of the outbuildings. We should check first.'

'Really? Rosewood? Wow, it would be fabulous to find them. I'll have a good look around. We haven't even looked in the garage, but it seems full of old bits and pieces. Perhaps there are some treasures in there we can re-use.'

As they walked through the building, Robbie took notes and measured as he went. They spent ages in the bathroom, while he measured the two bedrooms and sketched a new, bigger bathroom into his notepad. He understood the look she wanted to achieve and even suggested some money-saving tips to get it done.

After one last walk around the main room, they headed back to the front doors. Robbie stopped, touching her arm. She turned and looked at him as he pulled a neatly folded paper out of his back pocket. Handing it to her, he said, 'Our bill for the driveway. Harry did it for me last night. But he whinged the whole time, telling me our accounts are a mess.'

Nik looked at him, slightly surprised, and opened the bill. It was exactly what he had quoted. She nodded, refolded it and put it in her back pocket. 'I'll pay this today, Robbie, thank you. I still think it's cheap, you did all the drainage for free.'

'There's something else, Nik.' Again, she looked at him. He seemed nervous, and she nibbled at her bottom lip, suddenly feeling unsure of him. 'Would you be interested in doing a deal with me?'

'A deal?' she raised her eyebrows. She had not expected him to say that.

'Would you be interested in taking over our accounts, the bookkeeping for the business?'

'Yes, of course. I'd love to.' Knowing there was more, she waited.

'I'd give Lucy riding lessons in return. Not just riding lessons, but horsemanship lessons. However, many hours a week you need to be at my books, I will give lessons in return.'

'Wow! I didn't see that coming, but it's a perfect arrangement. In fact, I think Lucy and I will get the better end of this deal.' Grinning, she held out her hand. Robbie smiled back, taking her hand, and shaking it firmly. Her shoulders relaxed. He was genuine. Friend. Neighbour. Nothing more. Never anything more. But this was enough. Her steps were light as they headed back to the house.

9

And so it began. Robbie took his ute home that afternoon, but returned the next morning riding a large black gelding, leading a small grey mare, fully saddled, Scout trotting beside them. Lucy had seen him riding down the paddock from her bedroom and was out at the fence before he reached it.

'Good morning Cowboy Dad.' She waved and called out, before leaning down to pat Scout who promptly planted her backside on Lucy's foot.

He raised a hand in greeting. Stopping just a few metres from the fence, he said, 'This is Blackjack. He's the one I ride myself, so I'll ride him home this afternoon. The grey is Diana. She's sweet-natured, like Honey, but a little smaller. She might suit you better for a start.'

'Oh, really? She's very pretty.' Lucy was about to climb through the fence.

'Just a minute young lady.' He looked at her shorts and tee

shirt. 'Jeans and boots please. And let Mum know you're out here.'

'Okay!' Lucy sang out over her shoulder as she bolted inside to get changed, meeting Nik on the stairs. 'He's brought another horse. A smaller one. For me to ride. Her name's Diana.' Breathless, she disappeared into her room. Nik bounded down the stairs two at a time, herself dressed in shorts, tee shirt and canvas runners.

'Good morning!' She called out. He'd tied the big black horse up at the trough and was walking back to the fence, where the grey mare was quietly grazing.

'Morning Nik.' He smiled in welcome. 'Thought Diana here might suit Lucy better. I want to see if she can reach the stirrup to mount by herself.' He looked at Nik's shorts, grinning. 'I sent her in to get changed. Jeans and boots for horse riding.'

Nik looked down at her long, tanned legs, suddenly self-conscious. 'That's great. But just so you know, I'm not riding, so my attire is perfectly suitable.'

'I thought about that too. Wondered if you might like a riding lesson yourself. Honey would suit you. Then you can ride with Lucy once you both know the basics.' He was chuckling, looking really pleased with himself.

'Well. I don't know. I hadn't really thought about it.' Confused, she blushed and glanced over her shoulder. Lucy was dressed properly, and tearing across the grass toward them, Scout at her side.

He opened the fence for Lucy to climb through. 'Good girl.' He glanced at her laced-up hiking boots.

Nik watched as he introduced Lucy to Diana, in much the same way he had with Honey the day before. After a few minutes, he held the stirrup for Lucy to try. She got her toe in easily and bounded into the saddle with all the vigour of youth and enthusiasm. He handed Lucy the reins, showing her how to hold them. He led the little mare around holding the bridle, speaking quietly to Lucy, who listened intently. Nik sat on the grass with Scout, absorbing the lesson herself.

After half an hour, they came back to the fence. He helped Lucy unsaddle, remove the bridle, and let the horse go. She cantered back to the other horses, standing together at the trough, tossing her head as she went.

'Go and put the kettle on, Luce. We'll have a cuppa with Robbie.' Lucy skipped back to the house, the dog beside her. They watched as she patted Scout at the door, telling her to wait on the veranda. The dog did as she was told. Nik laughed, delighted.

'Thanks Nik. A cuppa will be lovely.' At the veranda, he turned and said, 'Lucy needs a riding hat, we don't have one the right size for her. Good if you got one too. And riding boots. The lace ups are okay for now but riding boots will be needed once she's riding on her own.'

Looking at the boots Robbie wore, Nik realised the difference. Yes, she would get hats and boots for them both. 'What you said before. About me learning to ride too. I'd like that, it's a great idea.' She smiled up at him. 'I don't think doing your accounts will really cover all of this.'

Laughing, he said, 'Wait until you see my accounts. They're a mess. I'm behind in everything ...'

Robbie mounted Blackjack. 'I won't be back today; I'm picking up supplies and quotes for the trades we need for the cottage.' Nik waved as he nudged the big horse into a slow canter, watching until horse and rider became small in the distance, grateful for this quietly spoken man, her neighbour and perhaps her friend.

Nik decided to drive into town, there was a saddlery that would sell riding hats and boots. She needed groceries too and wanted to drop in at Evans Real Estate to say hello. She asked Lucy if she wanted to come into town, try on boots and hats, pick up groceries and maybe grab a cold drink from the café. She was expecting a no, but Lucy nodded. 'I can do that, Mum. I'll come with you.'

While Lucy didn't speak to the people in the saddle shop, she happily tried on boots and hats. Walking to the café, they stopped at Evans Real Estate. Nik smiled to see her property in the window with a large red SOLD sign across it.

Lucy hovered behind Nik when Ben Evans stepped forward as they walked through the door. 'Nicola.' He held his hand out to take hers. Looking down at Lucy, he added, 'And you must be Lucy!' She nodded, not looking at him, but he didn't seem to mind.

'How are you settling in out there?' He offered them chairs in front of his desk, taking a seat himself.

'Please, call me Nik. Good actually. It's even better than we hoped. We've had some work done on the driveway by our neighbour, Robbie Stewart and his son, and he's quoting on some reno's for the cottage now.'

Ben nodded. 'Good man, Robbie. Hard workers, him, and his boy. He's fair too.'

'Yep. Lucky to have him next door. He's going to manage the trades too, which is a big help. But Lucy and I will do some of the smaller jobs, like sanding and painting.'

'And picking paint colours.' This from Lucy, who smiled shyly at Ben.

'Just as well. Most of us blokes are a bit colour blind, Lucy, much better that you and your Mum pick the colours.'

Nik leaned forward. 'I want to ask if you know much about the place. It's history? Robbie thinks there were solid rosewood doors on the front of the cottage at some point, but someone replaced them with cheap modern ones, and I'd love to get the original doors back, if they can be found. Do you think they were sold, or taken away? We haven't looked in the garage or sheds, it's possible they are still on the property.'

'Robbie's right. I remember those doors. There was a time they weren't appreciated, and they'd been painted over. More than once I should think.' He tapped a pencil on the desk, thinking. 'There's never been a clearing sale out there. Unless they were sold privately, you might find them in storage. If they've been kept in a dry place, they would be fine to sand back and refurbish.' He looked across at Nik. 'In fact, see what's still in those sheds. There may be good quality items you can sell, if you wish, or re-purpose. I'd have buyers if you find solid timber pieces you want to sell.'

Standing, Nik said 'Thank you Ben. I'll have a look at what's there. Perhaps you'd care to come out and see what we've got once we've unearthed everything?'

'Just let me know when you're ready. I'll come out and will bring Harriet Russell with me, she has an eye for good pieces.'

'Yes, Harriet. You know she found the place for me in the beginning. We wouldn't have come to this area if not for her.'

'Yes, I know. We're lucky to have her here. She's away for a few days, back in the big smoke, but I'll let her know you came in.' Ben walked them to the door, Lucy smiling at him as they left, her hand in Nik's.

As they strolled up the street, Nik gave her a wink. 'Nice work, Luce. You did well.'

'He is very tall, but nice. I think everyone in this town is nice, Mum. Not like city people.' Releasing her hand, Lucy gave a little skip. Nik nodded, but inwardly wondered how her daughter would cope if they met someone with an unpleasant manner, or scary personage.

10

The next few days passed quickly. Robbie arrived early each morning in his ute. Lucy would meet him at the laundry, already dressed in her riding gear to help him carry the tack out, bring Honey and Diana to the fence and brush them before they put the saddles on. Nik arrived in time for a lesson each day. Robbie walked them around in the paddock, at first adjusting stirrups and the way they held the reins. In just a few days they could ride to the trough and back on their own. Nik admitted she enjoyed it, not just to see Lucy so happy, and gaining confidence each day, but being in sync with Honey, feeling the power of the horse beneath her as she went from a walk to a trot with ease, responding to Nik's hands and knees like the pro that she was.

On the third morning, Robbie told Lucy she could bring the horses over and start brushing them. He had a building job to do. Nik stood on the doorstep, taking in the sight of him lifting a long post out of the back of his ute. She hurried over, taking one end of the post in her hands. 'Morning.' He grinned at her as she helped him carry it to the fence, before walking back to get a second, then a third one.

'Whew.' Nik wiped her forehead with the back of her hand. 'Heavy. What are we doing with these?'

'Well. I thought I'd set up a hitching rail inside the paddock. Safer to tie the horses up to and a bit away from the wire fence. With your permission, I'd like to set a timber gate in here too. Provide access into your place from mine.'

'Okay. Sounds good. Can I help?'

'Not really. I'm going to bring the tractor and post hole digger over, will set the two poles in first, then the pole between them. I'll do it this afternoon, just wanted to drop these off first.' He looked at Lucy, standing in the paddock, brushing Diana down. She had taken a piece of hay in with her, so the horses were content to chew as she brushed them. 'Smart girl.' He nodded to Nik.

'Born cowgirl, I think. Loves it here.' She turned to him, her smile wide. 'Thank you. The horses, and Scout, have done a lot for her. For both of us, actually.' Chuckling, she added, 'I've wrangled your accounts into order already. I've emailed the reports to you. I really think I owe you something. This deal is entirely in my favour.'

He touched her arm. 'It makes me happy to do it. I haven't enjoyed myself so much since… Well, since Jessica was alive, to tell the truth.'

It was the first time he had mentioned his wife since that first day, and Nik looked at him closely. His jaw was a little tense, but his smile reached his eyes. 'Thank you.' She leaned forward and kissed his cheek. It was barely a touch, a mere whisper, but the contact sent blood rushing to her face. And her nether regions. His eyes widened, as did his smile.

They both looked at Lucy, now busy brushing Honey. If she had seen the exchange, she didn't let on. 'Let them go when you're done there, Luce.' Robbie called out. She raised a hand to him. 'Okay!'

Looking at Nik, Robbie said, 'Harry will be over later. He's finished the other job. We're going to pull the existing kitchenette and bathroom out of the cottage. Removing the old tiles may take a bit of time. We want to set the frame for the expanded bathroom up tomorrow morning, as the plumber is due in the afternoon. I couldn't get Sandy Cooper, the local bloke, he's off until late January, having a break with his family over on the coast. I'm using Brandon Baxter, from Stroud, although he does a bit of work locally. His price is right, and I made enquiries about his work, but I really don't know him at all.' Robbie sounded apologetic.

'It's okay. I'm sure he'll be fine. Just pleased you're managing the trades. You know, keeping them honest. And I expected delays, so early in the New Year.' She smiled reassuringly.

Robbie continued. 'I thought I'd give you a hand to pull out some of the stuff in the old garage. We can lay it all out on the grass, check it out. Anything timber, or quality, we can put on the side veranda of the cottage for now, so you can sort through what might be worth keeping.'

'Oh, yes, sounds good. We opened the doors to the old garage the morning before last, intending to make a start. There were scrabbling noises in there. Not sure what it was. Possum, rats, snake?' Nik shuddered. 'I'd feel so much better if you helped us make a start, make sure there's nothing, ugh, *poisonous* in there.' She took a step back.

'May be a possum, but more likely mice. Once we start moving stuff, we'll flush them out.' He didn't mention snakes, but Nik knew it was a very real possibility.

'We might leave our jeans and boots on for this, I think.' She smiled grimly at him. He laughed, touching her shoulder. 'You'll be fine.'

'Quick breakfast first? Lucy has oranges to squeeze, and I'll scramble some eggs on to a bit of toast for us.' Nik inclined her head, smiling.

'Lovely. You're lovely.' He looked across at Lucy, leaving the horses to their hay, Scout trotting beside her. 'I'd love to have breakfast with you. With both of you.'

THE GARAGE DOORS CAME OPEN EASIER THAN THEY HAD FOR NIK. The day was already warm, but Nik kept her boots on, with gardening gloves at the ready, and made sure Lucy did the same. There were pieces of timber, old bed frames, ancient farm equipment, piled almost to the ceiling.

'I reckon this calls for gloves, Luce.' Nik pulled on her own. 'Yuk.' Lucy followed suit. Robbie chuckled.

'I'll climb up, pass some of these pieces down from on top. Let me know if anything is too heavy, and I'll jump down.' Robbie climbed up onto the pile and rummaged about. He passed down a few long pieces of timber, which Nik managed to take, and with Lucy's help stacked them into a pile on the grass outside. Next came a bedhead, then the rest of the bed frame.

'That timber is Australian cedar. We might be able to do something with that,' Robbie called down. Next, he passed down section after section of wrought iron lacework, paint-chipped but in good condition. She held a piece up in front of her, each section was about a metre wide. 'Is this from a veranda do you think?'

'The upstairs veranda on the house had wrought iron lacework at one stage, but a long time ago. You could put it back there, but I think it could work nicely around the veranda of the cottage.'

Lucy looked at the piece Nik was holding. 'Could we do that, Mum?'

'We could paint it white; it would set off the colour we've chosen for the outside walls nicely.' Nik turned the piece as she studied it. 'If there's enough, but if there's not we could just use it on the front part, that people see.' Nik was pleased. She could sand it back and she and Lucy could paint it, so it wouldn't cost anything, really, and it would look great on the cottage.

Robbie started laughing. 'Wait 'til you see what's in here, girls.' He handed down piece after piece of wrought iron. 'There's enough for the whole veranda of the cottage. This would have been around the top and bottom of the house, originally.'

'I'm tempted to put it back around the house, but the upstairs balcony has cleaner lines now. So maybe keep it at the cottage. Either way, we'll use it. What a find.'

Robbie had moved further into the garage, now passing out old tractor seats and rusty farm equipment. Nik couldn't see any use for it, except perhaps as garden ornaments. But she didn't want the place to look kitschy. By mid-morning they had a pile of junk, and another pile of good pieces they could re-purpose. Lucy had gone to the house, bringing back bottles of cold water and a plate of carrot cake. She stayed out the front of the house, playing under the plum tree with Scout, who seemed to be moving more sluggishly.

Robbie stood beside Nik for a moment. 'I think she's due in about a week, maybe two. Could be sooner. She'll lay down in the shade there and rest. Lucy's worked hard with us this morning.' He turned to Nik. 'How old is she? Lucy, I mean. She's quite tall, like you, but I'm guessing about twelve.'

'Eleven, not twelve for another six months. Yes, Lucy is going to be tall, I think.' She looked up at Robbie, standing well over six foot. 'Tall for a woman, that is. I'm five-nine. She might make my height.'

He smiled at her. 'Most kids that age won't stay and help as long as she did. Harry used to disappear after about half an hour unless it was tractor work.' As he spoke, Harry's ute came slowly up the driveway. 'Speak of the devil.' He chuckled, but Nik clearly saw the pride on his face as his strapping son stepped out of his car. He paused at the plum tree, speaking briefly with Lucy, patting Scout, then sauntered across to them.

'Hey Dad. Hi Nik.' He looked at the pile of wrought iron pieces. 'Awesome! Looks like you've found buried treasure in here. Want a hand? Or should we start with the bathroom demolition?' He looked from Nik to his father.

'Another half-hour here, with the three of us, would be perfect.' Nik was enthusiastic and excited to see if there was anything else of value hidden in the old building.

Harry immediately jumped up on the pile, now much lower, and began handing things out to them. 'Oh wow! Hey Nik,' he called, 'there's a lovely old chest of drawers in here, and an old kitchen dresser. Dusty, but doesn't look damaged.'

Robbie waded back in, carrying the two pieces out with Harry. Nik pounced on them. 'The drawers are beautiful.' She opened a couple, running her hands over the timber. 'Is this walnut, do you think?' Robbie had a close look, pulled a whole drawer out and scratched the inside gently.

'Better than walnut. This is rosewood. Sand it back and oil it, the lustre and grain will be stunning. I think it could be more than a hundred years old. Look at the way it's made, all tongue and groove. Beautiful craftsmanship.'

'Oh. What a find. I can't believe it. It would be perfect in the cottage, but I'd love it in my room in the house.' Nik walked from the drawers to the kitchen dresser. 'And this. Stunning. Needs a bit of work too, but how lovely. Also, for the house, I think.' Lucy had wandered over and was busily opening the drawers in the dresser. One small one was stuck. 'Mum, this one is stuck.'

'Don't force it. It may be swollen.' Harry stepped over. 'Let me try.' He pulled at the drawer, tugging gently, then looked underneath. 'There are some papers in the drawer, and one is stuck in the back.' He slid the drawer out about an inch, then slipped two fingers in, pushing the papers down a bit, then inched the drawer out further. After several attempts it was open, and Lucy fell on the contents.

'Be careful, the papers will be old.' Nik looked over her shoulder. Freeing a couple of pieces, tied up with string through a hole in the corner, Lucy turned around, eyes shining. 'They're recipes. Really old recipes.' She gently pulled the bundle out, then reached in, bringing more bundles out, then a couple of envelopes. Turning to them, she commanded, 'Don't touch these, I'm going to get some plastic sleeves from Mum's office to put them in, they're very fragile.'

'Yes ma'am.' Harry grinned at her as she shot off. Looking at Nik, he said, 'we're nearly done, I'm going to see what else is at the back. There's something leaning against the back wall that looks a bit like old doors.'

She nodded eagerly as the two men rummaged around behind an old tractor body, eventually emerging, carrying a large door between them. They strode back in and returned with another, leaning them against the chest of drawers, before grinning in unison at Nik.

'Are these what I think they are?' She rubbed the dust off a section of the door. 'They're so thick. And heavy.'

Harry, dust in his hair, slapped Robbie on the back. 'Yup, they are. Not just the original doors of the cottage. They're the original courthouse doors. Solid rosewood, they'll be beautiful after they've been sanded and polished.'

Nik laughed, but threw a questioning look at the two men. 'How do you know they're the original courthouse doors?'

Robbie laughed and turned over the door nearest to him. Rubbing with his elbow, he cleaned an old brass plaque in the centre. Nik leant closer. *Barrington Courthouse, 1891.*

She hugged them, first Harry, then Robbie, before calling out to Lucy who was walking back from the house with plastic folders in her hand. 'Luce! See what we've got!'

Running the last few metres Lucy had a look. 'Wow!' She hugged Nik. 'Do you think we should put them on the house, though?'

'No, I don't. They would have been on the top part, with external stairs going up to the courthouse. The stairs have long since gone. No, I think they're perfect for the cottage. It's just what we hoped to find. I can't imagine why anyone would have replaced them in the first place!'

Robbie raised his eyebrows. 'Remember all those solid timber kitchens our grandparents had in the sixties? Replaced by bright orange and green Formica in the seventies? And solid timber tables replaced by laminate ones? Fashion trends. Not always good.'

He looked around, at the pieces on the ground, and leaning against furniture. 'There are a couple of old tractors still in there. I suggest we stack the pieces back in that you don't want. There is a second-hand store in town. They'll come out with a truck and take what you don't need, you might even get a bit of cash for some of it.'

Nodding, Nik glanced around. 'Good. Thanks. I'll call them today. But all the wrought iron, the furniture, and those doors. I need to store them safely for now, away from the cottage while the work is going on.'

'How about downstairs in the house. The back bedrooms. If you're not going to work on those until the cottage is finished, that may be the place. We can make some room around the chest of drawers, the kitchen dresser and the doors, so we can get to them for sanding and polishing.' Robbie nodded at Harry, who was already lifting pieces of wrought iron. 'We'll get the good stuff safely away first, son. The rest can lay out here today, it's likely they'll come and look at it tomorrow.'

Nik and Lucy began to work with them, carrying the lighter timber pieces back to the house. They laid everything on the ground, letting the men stack it inside in a sensible manner. Lucy chatted as she went, occasionally asking Robbie, or Harry a question about a particular piece. What it was used for, how old it was. She was no longer shy or reticent with them.

Nik hadn't felt so happy in a long time. Every now and again she met Robbie's eyes, to find him looking at her, amusement clear on his face. Once, when she passed him a piece of timber, his hand touched hers. She blushed and looked at him quickly. Robbie stood still for a moment, the muscle in his jaw twitching slightly. Taken aback Nik looked away and kept working.

11

F aint beams of sunlight tumbled through the window,
waking Nik just after dawn. Stretching, she yawned
and threw back the sheet. The night had been warm.
Clad only in singlet and knickers, she padded through to Lucy's
room. The bed was empty, the covers pulled up haphazardly.
Smiling, Nik went back to the window in her room that over-
looked Robbie's paddock. Lucy was down there, feeding hay to
the mares.

Capturing her hair in a high ponytail, Nik threw on her jeans
from yesterday, with a bra and clean tank top. She added canvas
runners. Nik didn't think they'd have time for a riding lesson
today, as they hadn't finished the demolition in the cottage
yesterday and the plumber was due mid-morning.

Hurrying downstairs, she noted her legs and shoulders
were stiff and sore from yesterday's exertions. Lucy walked
through the door, smiling happily. 'Morning, Mum. I've fed the
horses. Robbie and Harry are already in the cottage and he said

he'd give me a lesson this afternoon, after the plumber has been.'

'Good girl. Can you pop some toast in while I dash over and see if the men need anything?' Nik was out the door as she spoke, but she saw Lucy nod while taking her boots off.

The front doors had been taken off the cottage and all the windows and doors were open. Dust swirled around in the main room, the men wearing masks over their nose and mouth, oblivious she had arrived as they ripped up tiles in the kitchen section, the old cupboards and stove already gone.

Stepping closer, she covered her mouth and nose with her hand. Robbie looked up, saw her, and reached out to tap Harry on the shoulder, who looked up and stopped his work too.

'Morning, Nik. Don't stay in here while we're doing this, at least not without a mask.' Robbie straightened as he spoke, pulling his mask down, flashing a quick smile in her direction.

'Morning Nik.' Harry echoed, putting his tools down and stretching his arms over his head.

'You started early. Thanks so much.' She stepped closer. 'Have you had breakfast? I can bring some toasted sandwiches out, or you can come back to the house.'

'We had something at home before we left.' Robbie gestured towards the floor, more than half of the tiles already removed. 'The bathroom's done and we removed the walls to the bedrooms yesterday, just leaving the main studs and beams in place until we're ready to put the new walls in.' He wiped his eyes with the back of his arm, leaving a smear of dirt across his forehead. 'I reckon we'll be done here in another hour. If it's okay with you and Lucy, we'll come over and have a cuppa with you then. After that Harry will take some of this rubbish to the tip. The plumber, Baxter, should be here by then.'

'Great. Come over when you're ready. Is there anything we can do here to help?' Nik looked around, it was mostly done, and the last bit required plenty of strength.

'Thanks, but we've got this covered. I've left a plan of your proposed new bathroom on the front seat of the ute. Can you get it out and have a look? I want to make sure you're happy with it before we get Baxter to locate the pipes.' Nik nodded as he added 'It's not a problem to move things around if you want to reconfigure it.'

'Okay, I'll grab it, we'll have a look while you're finishing this bit.' Nik turned to leave, then turned back. 'Is Scout with you today? I didn't see her as I came over?'

Robbie stood, looked at Harry for a moment, who raised his eyebrows in surprise. 'She came with us. She's close to having the pups, she might just be laying somewhere cool. Can you please check on her, but come back if you can't find her? I don't want her getting under the house or somewhere it'll be hard to get her out of, if she's ready to whelp.'

Nodding, Nik hurried back to the house, checking in the shed first, then under the plum tree. Lucy was on the veranda. 'Have you seen Scout?' She shook her head but started to pull her boots back on. 'Can you lay down and look under the house, Luce?' Worried, Nik bit her lip, wondering where else the dog may be resting. The noise and dust in the cottage would keep her away from there, but she usually lay on the veranda or under the plum tree during the day.

Standing up, Lucy shook her head. 'She's not under there, Mum. Have you checked she's not in the shed we worked on yesterday? Nik nodded. 'We'll find her. Robbie said she might be looking for somewhere quiet and cool to have her pups.'

Standing still Lucy looked at Nik, her mouth a round 'O'

shape. 'Her pups? You think she'll have them here? At our house?' She was delighted.

'Maybe. He thinks they're due any day now.'

'The laundry!' Lucy shot around the side of the house, Nik right behind her. The laundry door was closed, and Scout was nowhere about.

'I'll go over to Robbie. They'll have to help us look.' Nik left Lucy on the veranda, jogging back to the cottage. She returned a few minutes later, Robbie and Harry on her heels. Lucy wasn't where she had left her, but perhaps she'd gone upstairs.

'Scout may have headed for home, perhaps back through the paddock. I'll take one of the horses and look that way.' Robbie turned to Harry. 'Can you go back to the shed, she might've gone right inside, under one of the tractors.' About to head their separate ways, Lucy appeared, a happy smile on her face.

'I've found her. I called to her when Mum ran across to the cottage. She was right here the whole time.' She gestured inside the house. 'The front door has been open all morning, since I got up to feed the horses.' They followed her inside, to Nik's little office.

Looking under the desk, they found Scout, curled up on a cardigan Nik had left on the back of her chair days ago, which had fallen to the floor. Lucy had pulled the chair out, and was down on her haunches, speaking quietly to Scout.

Robbie knelt beside her. 'Hey girl, are you ready to have your babies?' He reached in, scratching Scout behind the ears. He was about to slide her out from under the desk, on the cardigan, when Harry, who was laying on the floor now, half under the desk, help up his hand. 'Stop, Dad. We can't move her now. Have a look.'

Harry shimmied out and Robbie took his place. He shuffled

to one side. 'Lucy, come under here, Have a look.' Lucy didn't hesitate, dropping to the floor and crawling under the desk, right beside Robbie. Nik tried to peer in, but it was dark under there. 'Oh, there's one already! No two!' Lucy's excitement was evident, although she was trying to whisper.

Robbie backed out and stood up. 'Sorry Nik. She's started whelping. I'd rather not move her just yet. But, um, your cardigan …'

Nik touched his arm. 'It doesn't matter. It's an old one. What can we do to help her?'

Lucy backed out. 'Now there's three. She's licking them. They're tiny and their eyes are closed.' She was breathless with excitement.

'We need to bring her water bowl in here, and one of us needs to stay with her. She'll let us know if she's in trouble. She'll yelp or get agitated.' Robbie looked at Lucy. 'What do you say, Lucy, do you want to sit with her, make sure she has water and tell us if you think she's upset?'

Nodding wordlessly, Lucy shot outside, returning with the water bowl, half full, in her hands. She slowly slid it under the desk, where Scout could reach it. Wagging her tail, she lapped at the water for a moment, her eyes thanking Lucy. 'There's four now!' Lucy slid back out.

Nik dropped to her knees, reached under, and patted Scout gently. 'Okay, Luce. You stay here. I'll bring some toast down for you and an orange juice. I'll be nearby too.'

'How many will she have Mum?' Nik turned to Robbie, who shook his head slightly. 'Hard to say, this could be it, just four, but she could have seven or eight.'

'She seems okay though. Not upset or having trouble?' Nik frowned a little as she asked.

'It's her second litter. She had four last time, no problem at all. Best just to have someone nearby, she'll let us know if she needs help.' Robbie smiled reassuringly, before moving back to the veranda where Harry was already putting his boots on. 'We'll be over for that cuppa in less than an hour. She should be done by then. But come and get me if you need to.' He put his boots on, nudged Harry, who nudged him back, laughing, then strode off toward the cottage, his son by his side.

Nik went back to Lucy. 'Five now Mummy. Scout is licking them all. They are crawling around near her tummy.'

'Okay, sweetheart. I'll fix us some breakfast and we can sit down here and have it while we keep an eye on Scout and her puppies.'

Less than ten minutes later, Nik was navigating her way down the stairs, a plate of toast in one hand and a glass of juice in the other. About to set them on her desk, Lucy cried out. 'One of them isn't moving Mum! Quick, get Robbie. It's really small. Smaller than the others. It's number seven!' Lucy sounded distressed. Nik dumped the items she was carrying on the earnest surface and slid under beside Lucy. Scout was licking the tiny pup, but it wasn't moving at all. She nudged it toward Nik and Lucy. Nik reached out, speaking softly to the dog. 'We'll have a look at your baby, Scout. Don't worry.'

Nik had the puppy in her hand, sliding out from under the desk she sat up, Lucy beside her, starting to cry. 'Don't let it die, Mummy, do something.'

Nik held the puppy up, sticky stuff covering its mouth and nose. Afterbirth, she thought, this is what Scout was trying to lick off. She pulled up the hem of her tank top and gently cleaned the mucus from the tiny pup's face and mouth. It didn't move. She gently prised its mouth open, putting her finger in, cleared more of the stuff out. It still didn't move, and Scout was starting to whimper. Lucy stood. 'I'm getting Robbie!' She ran from the room, crying.

Nik wiped a tear from her eye as she placed the little pup close to Scout. 'I'm sorry. I don't think this one is going to make it.' She watched, crying softly as Scout licked and nudged the pup. Hearing footsteps on the veranda, she turned as Robbie came in. He put a hand on her shoulder. 'This happens sometimes, with a big litter.'

He slid under the desk, talking to Scout quietly. Moments later he was back out, smiling at Nik and Lucy. 'Have a look.'

They shimmied under, the littlest pup was moving its head, searching for a nipple at Scout's belly with its siblings. Scout thumped her tail against the floor, a doggy smile on her face.

Nik came back out, leaving Lucy to watch. She stood, and Robbie put his arms around her, holding her tight for a moment. 'Lucy told me you cleared the mucus off its face, even out of its mouth. You saved it, Nik, good job.'

Smiling through her tears, she stepped back, but felt a brief sense of loss as Robbie released her from his embrace.

12

The sound of a vehicle driving in sent them outside. A large grey van, *Baxter Plumbing* across the side and rear doors, drove over to the cottage.

Robbie and Nik walked across together while Harry stepped out from the cottage. Brendan Baxter was a solid man, not as tall as Robbie, but broader through the shoulders, hips, and legs. He had a strong face, large nose, prominent jaw. Handsome in an obvious sort of way, Nik thought.

He greeted the men with a handshake but brazenly looked Nik up and down before taking her outstretched hand by just her fingertips, giving a quick shake. She frowned. It was one of her pet hates when men wouldn't shake a woman's hand properly. He made her uncomfortable, his look intense, almost a leer.

Robbie stepped forward and she could tell he wasn't impressed either. 'Just in here, Brendan. Can you confirm the price you gave based on the plans I emailed through?' Directing him inside, Nik wasn't sure if she should stay, or just leave it to Robbie.

Harry followed them in then popped back out to Nik. 'Dad says you might want to see if the second-hand bloke can come out for a look at the stuff in the old shed today, or tomorrow. He doesn't think you need to hang around for the plumbing.'

Nodding, Nik said quietly, 'Thanks, Harry. I'll give them a call now. And I also told Ben Evans I'd give him a call. If Harriet Russell is back from Sydney, they might want to have a look too.'

Back at the house Nik checked on Lucy and Scout. Seven was the magic number, and all the puppies were feeding while Scout lay back. Lucy had given her more water but wasn't sure what else she should do. 'Just stay nearby I think, Lucy.' Nik hesitated. 'The plumber is here. Um, Luce, just stay away from the cottage okay? He's not like Robbie and Harry.'

Lucy looked startled but nodded. Nik went upstairs and changed from her figure-hugging tank top to an old, baggy tee shirt, which she left out over her jeans. Baxter's eyes had roved over her body, making her feel uncomfortable. She wasn't going to give him anything to look at in the future.

About an hour later, they heard footsteps on the veranda. Nik walked out, cautiously. It was Robbie. 'You alright?' He looked at Nik with concern. If he noticed her change of top, he didn't mention it.

'Sure. I hope his work is better than his manner with customers.'

'Agreed. If Sandy wasn't away until the end of the month, I'd send Baxter packing. He was rude, Nik. I'm sorry.'

'Not your fault. But I don't want him near Lucy.' Nik spoke

quietly, glancing over her shoulder to make sure Lucy was out of earshot.

'Harry's going to hang around in the cottage while he's here, do a bit of work on the new walls.' Robbie didn't have to add that Harry wasn't going to let the plumber come near the house, but Nik knew that's what he meant. She was grateful. Just meeting him had her nerves on edge. He was exactly the personality type that would terrify Lucy.

'Thank you.' She gave Robbie a small smile. Lucy popped out, a wide smile stretched across her face. 'There's seven puppies. Minnie was the last one.'

'Minnie?' Robbie and Nik spoke together.

'She's smaller than the others.' Lucy sounded defensive but couldn't seem to take the smile off her face.

'Minnie she is then.' Robbie gave Lucy a quick grin as he spoke. 'I'll check on them, then we might leave Mum with them while we have a riding lesson.'

'Oh, good. I'll get my boots.' Lucy rushed upstairs. They moved into the study. 'We need to move Scout from here, but I'm not sure about taking her home today. Do you think she could stay in the downstairs laundry for a few days, until the pups are a bit stronger? And just so you know, Minnie may get pushed around by the bigger pups. Natural selection kicks in with a big litter, and I may have to hand feed her if she weakens.'

'Oh, I didn't know that. About the pups.' Nik clarified. 'And yes, I'm happy for her to be here. What can I set up in the laundry to make it comfortable for her?'

'An old blanket or a couple of towels will be good if you have them. I can shoot home and bring her normal bedding back with me later, and some food for her.' Lucy reappeared, all geared up and ready. 'I'll take Lucy for a lesson, then we'll see if Scout's ready to move when we get back.'

'I'll stay here. I've got to do a load of washing, and I'll move things around in the laundry to make a cosy spot for her.' Nik and Robbie exchanged quick smiles as they watched Lucy hurry toward the horses.

IT WAS ALMOST TWO HOURS LATER WHEN LUCY REAPPEARED, HER face pink with excitement. 'I went for a proper ride. Not on the lead rope, but *by myself*!' She emphasised the last two words, adding, 'we rode all the way to Robbie's house. Well, not quite, but we could see it in the distance. And there was a paddock with Blackjack and other horses. He has a lot of horses!'

'Wow! You're really doing well. Where's Robbie now?' Nik looked past Lucy, in the doorway, but couldn't see him.

'He went over to the cottage to check on the work. He helped me unsaddle, then I brushed them and fed them by myself.'

'Good girl. How about you run up and take a shower, put some clean clothes on. You smell like a horse.' Nik wrinkled her nose, laughing.

THE AFTERNOON WORE ON. NIK HAD CALLED BEN EVANS. HE AND Harriet were going to come out at ten the next morning to check out the pieces they'd found in the old garage, see if any of it was worth selling. She was looking forward to seeing Harriet again. She was younger than Nik but had lived in Sydney for a long time and now had a good life and thriving business out here, helping people like herself relocate to the region.

It was late in the afternoon when she saw the plumber drive out in his van. She breathed a sigh of relief. He really had unnerved her. Lucy was sitting cross-legged a few metres from where Scout lay with her puppies, reading quietly. Nik had told her to stop handling the puppies, to let them feed and rest. Scout seemed rested too.

Robbie and Harry appeared on the veranda.

'How'd it go?' Nik looked from one to the other.

'There's more to do, once we get the walls set and ready to put the fixtures in. But that won't be until later next week.' Robbie looked at Harry, then Nik. 'We won't use him for the work we do here, in the house, later on. Sandy Cooper will be back for that.'

Harry added, 'His work is fine, I really can't fault anything he's done today. But I've seen him in the pub a few times. He gets a bit aggressive after a beer or two. Dad's right, you don't need tradies like that hanging around.'

They took their boots off and came in to visit Scout and the puppies. Robbie explained to Harry and Lucy that they should stay for a few days, but they needed to move them to the laundry.

'I've put down an old blanket, and a towel, and made a bit of a nest in the corner behind the door for her.' Nik put her arm around Lucy. 'What's the best way to move them in there?'

'We'll get Lucy to take Minnie, and we'll each pick up two pups. I'll call Scout and she'll follow us in.'

Lucy shimmied under the counter, speaking softly to Scout. After patting her gently she picked up Minnie, cradling her against her chest.

Robbie called Scout to him, and she quietly stood, and walked out, looking behind at the pups that were all bundled together, crawling over each other and whimpering. Harry slid Nik's cardigan out, the pups huddled together on it. He handed a pup each to Nik and Robbie and scooped the rest up in the cardigan. Robbie picked up the water bowl and they walked around to the laundry on the veranda, Scout right beside Lucy all the way.

They settled Scout on the blanket and gently placed all the pups against her belly, where they immediately squirmed and nudged each other, seeking a nipple to feed from. Robbie put the water bowl down close to her head. Harry had the cardigan in his hand. 'I'll take this home and wash it Nik.'

She laughed and took it from his hand. 'We're in a laundry right now. I'll rinse it, then soak it. But if it can't be saved, I'll put it back in with Scout once it's dry.'

'Will I put the kettle on, Mum?' Lucy asked.

'How about a beer, boys? I bought some when I went into town. I think we should celebrate the new arrivals.' She raised her eyebrows in question.

'I won't say no.' Harry laughed. 'Show me where the fridge is Lucy; we'll get the drinks. Do you want one too, Nik?'

'Sure. And Lucy you can have a coke.' Harry followed Lucy out, while Nik and Robbie continued to watch the pups. Nik turned to speak to Robbie but noted a look of concern on his face. She looked back at the dogs.

'What is it?'

'The little one, Minnie. The bigger pups are pushing her away and she isn't getting a feed. If she doesn't drink soon, she might not make it until morning. Nik, I hope you don't mind, but I need to stay here overnight to hand feed her. I don't want to lose her; Lucy is already so attached.'

Surprised, she looked at the puppies again. Robbie was right. Every time Minnie latched onto a nipple one of the bigger puppies pushed her out of the way. Scout gave her a few licks but seemed resigned to the situation.

'Of course, you can stay. I'll sit up with you, we can take it in turns to feed her. How do we do it, I really have no idea.'

'Warm milk and an eyedropper. Her tummy is tiny, she needs milk every couple of hours.'

Lucy and Harry returned, handing around drinks while Robbie explained the situation. Harry nodded. 'I'll go home and get a few things for Scout, and for you Dad for the morning. After that I'll pick up pizzas from the pub, if it's okay with the girls, we can all eat here tonight.'

'Yes. Good thinking, son.' Robbie turned to Nik and then Lucy. 'Does this work for you?' They both nodded but Nik didn't miss his real concern and added 'Yes, of course.'

HARRY LEFT AT NINE, HAVING EATEN A WHOLE PIZZA WASHED DOWN with two beers. Lucy helped feed Minnie twice, then Nik sent her to bed, promising she would wake her if the tiny pup wasn't doing well.

'Why don't you go to bed too, Nik? I'll feed her again at midnight, then two in the morning. We should know by then if she'll make it.' Robbie smiled tiredly at Nik.

She looked at him. He had arrived at dawn and worked hard all day. He must be exhausted. 'I'll sit up with you. If you doze off, I'll feed her. I want her to live as much as you do.'

So, they sat, on the floor of the laundry, backs against the wall, occasionally chatting. Robbie told Nik about his early life camp drafting, then meeting Jessica when he was nineteen. 'Harry's age. We were married inside two years. She worked in childcare, but once Harry came along, we bought the farm, and she helped run it while I ran the building business. It was my father's and I had completed an apprenticeship before I went on the camp draft circuit. At the time I wasn't keen to take over the business, but having a wife and child changed all that. By the time I was twenty-five I was running it with Dad. He died when Harry was twelve.' Robbie looked down. 'I miss him every day. Almost as much as Jess. And Isobel.'

'Isobel?' Nik saw raw pain in Robbie's eyes.

'Our little girl. She only lived three weeks. Born early, too tiny. Her lungs never fully developed.' He looked at Nik, raw emotion etched into his face. 'She'd be twelve now. Close to Lucy's age.'

13

The catch in his voice, pain on his face, made Nik reach for him. They were sitting side by side. She took his face, leaned in, and gently kissed his cheek. He moved his head and caught the edge of her mouth with his. Closing her eyes, Nik moved her mouth against his. It was a tender kiss, full of promise, but she forced herself to break contact.

'Nik?' his voice was gravelly, his need clear.

Shaking her head, she swallowed a sob. 'I can't Robbie. You're lovely. Warm, gentle, strong. But I can't.'

He took her hand in his, but she pulled away. 'What happened to you Nik? To you and Lucy? Who hurt you? Let me understand.' But she shook her head.

'I will tell you. One day. But you need to know it was my fault. It was all my fault. I made a terrible choice. I chose some-one, after my marriage ended. A long time after. We were on our own for five years. I fell for him. Trusted him. Quickly. Too quickly. By the time I realised he wasn't who I thought he was, it was too late. The damage was done.' She angrily swiped tears from her eyes with the back of her hand, ignoring Robbie's look of sympathy. 'He hurt us. Physically. Emotionally. It can never be undone. Never be forgotten. But we're learning to live with it. These last couple of weeks have been amazing. Lucy gaining confidence. You, Harry, Scout. The horses. But Robbie, I promised her I would never let a man into our lives again. Into our family. Friendship is all I can offer.'

He withdrew his hand and nodded, leaning his head back against the wall. 'I understand, Nik. I haven't been interested in anyone since I lost Jessica. And you are lovely. And there's Lucy. I imagine Isobel would have been like her, crazy about horses and dogs. Gentle. Smart.' He nudged her gently with his shoulder. 'But I can be friends. Friendship is good. Strong. Friendship will last. You're okay with me Nik. I won't push.'

Looking at him in the dim light, hearing the sincerity in his voice, the affection, she almost caved and reached for him. But she'd promised Lucy. She smiled, not sure if he could see her expression. 'We'll be great friends, Robbie. I'm so lucky we have you and Harry in our lives.'

Scout raised her head, then stood. Robbie scrambled to his feet. 'I think she needs to go outside for a minute. I'll take her if you can watch the pups.'

Nik scooted closer to the pups, who were sleeping together like a big bundle of wriggly fur.

SHE WOKE WHEN ROBBIE GENTLY TOUCHED HER ARM. THE SUN WAS coming up, and the puppies were squirming against Scout's belly. She looked at them, thumping her tail on the floor a few times. He reached over, extracting Minnie from the bundle. They had last fed her at two. He turned her over, her little tummy was as tight as a drum.

'She's had a feed by herself. I watched her shove one of the bigger ones away about an hour ago. I think she'll be okay.' They smiled tiredly at each other as he gently placed the pup against her mother.

Lucy appeared in the doorway, still in her pyjamas. 'Is Minnie okay?' she whispered.

'Come and see.' Nik held out her arms and Lucy plonked down on her lap, looking closely at Scout and the puppies.

'Oh, look Robbie, she's drinking by herself. That's good, isn't it?' Lucy looked hopefully at Robbie.

'It sure is. She's a determined little thing.' He cleared his throat. 'You know the pups won't open their eyes until they're about ten days old?'

Lucy nodded. 'I looked that up on google last night.'

Robbie continued. 'We're going to be here almost every day for the next couple of weeks. If it's alright with you and Mum, I think Scout and the pups should stay here. She'd be alone during the day at home, but here she has you to look after her.'

'Can we, Mum? Can we keep them here? I promise to look after her and clean up after the pups.' Lucy screwed up her nose, then pointed to the damp mess on the old towel.

'It's a great idea. And I'll help you. If you can show me, and Robbie, how responsible you are with them, he might let us keep Minnie when she's old enough to be weaned.' Robbie and Nik had talked about it during the night and agreed that Lucy could have Minnie.

'For real? True?' Lucy hugged her mother, then threw herself into Robbie's arms, giving him a giant hug, before scooting over to the pups and extracting Minnie for a cuddle. Robbie was surprised, and moved, by Lucy's show of affection.

Standing, he walked to the laundry door, looking out at the horses in the paddock nearby. 'Let's get the horses fed Lucy, then I'll have a quick shower and change.'

Nik joined them at the door. 'There's a fresh towel in the bathroom upstairs and I'll whip up some scrambled eggs on toast. It's been a long night.'

14

Harry arrived, and although he said he'd had breakfast at home, tucked into a serve of scrambled eggs too. Lucy dragged him to the laundry to show him how well the pups were doing. It was amazing how comfortable Lucy was with him. Like a big brother. Nik swallowed a lump in her throat, stealing a look at Robbie. He was staring at the doorway, where the kids had been a moment before. Turning, he looked at her, his eyes dark with emotion, and pain. Breaking his gaze, he took his plate to the sink.

Gathering herself, she cleared the rest of the table. 'I'll do these. You've been working every day for the last couple of weeks. Are you sure you wouldn't like to take the day off, spend some time at home? Catch up on some sleep?'

'And do what? Harry fed the stock at home this morning. We can get those new walls up today, and I'd like to be here when Ben and Harriet come to look at the pieces we found. We might call it a day after that, if you and Lucy are fine with Scout and the puppies.'

Nik washed and Robbie dried. The horses were in clear view from the kitchen window. Harry carried some hay over, Lucy beside him with a brush in each hand. It was obvious they were talking, while they brushed the two mares. Then Harry put the brushes on the top of a fence post, picked up some straw from the hay bundle and threw it at Lucy, before taking off toward the trough. She raced after him, laughing. She chased him around the trough twice, then reached in and flicked water at him. He flicked her back, then chased her to the fence. With his long legs, he could have caught her twice over, but he stayed just behind while she squealed in mock terror.

Nik looked at Robbie. He just nodded at the window. 'He's a good lad. Good-natured. But he'll fire up if someone, or something, is unjust or unfair. Got into a few scraps at school, but generally he was standing up for a mate. Can't criticise him for that.' Hanging the tea towel in front of the oven, Robbie turned to Nik. 'He took it hard when his mother died, he was only fifteen, but in a way, it's made us closer.' She glanced out the window, Lucy and Harry were no longer in sight. She nodded her understanding.

A bellow from downstairs made them laugh out loud. 'Hey Dad, are you going to come and finish this job in the cottage, or are you up there baking cakes or something?' They heard Lucy giggle. Then Harry added, more quietly, 'Honestly, the only thing Dad can cook is steak on the barbecue. Or sausages. Oh, and chops and bacon. We'd starve to death if it weren't for me; and Debbie's café in town.' Harry laughed again, Lucy giggling with him.

Grinning, Robbie called back. 'I heard that, Harry Stewart. Be prepared to work up a sweat because we're going to finish the bathroom walls this morning!'

'And I'll bake you a cake!' Lucy's girlish voice rang out.

'Excellent, Luce. I was hoping you'd say that.' Harry's voice was light and teasing.

'Behave, Harry Stewart, or you won't have any cake,' Lucy responded, using Harry's full name like Robbie had, making Nik snort with laughter. Robbie grinned, winked at Nik then ran downstairs, two at a time.

Nik checked on the puppies, filled Scout's water bowl and gave her the dog food Harry had brought from home. Leaving the laundry door ajar so she could slip out if she needed to, they went back to the kitchen upstairs. Lucy baked a carrot cake while Nik made another big batch of lemonade.

At exactly ten, Ben and Harriet arrived in a modern Range Rover with *Evans Real Estate* lettering on the doors. Harriet was small and slim, with thick honey blonde hair, dressed in capri pants and a loose cotton peasant top, canvas runners on her feet. Lucy smiled shyly as they walked out to greet them, standing back a bit until Harriet asked her what the delicious smell was. 'Have you or Mum been baking, Lucy?'

'I have. Carrot cake for morning tea.' She looked up at Harriet, adding, 'Mum made lemonade. From our own lemons. It's for you and Mr Evans. And Robbie and Harry.'

'I knew a morning visit was a good idea.' Harriet nudged Ben, who smiled warmly down at Lucy.

Nik led them to the old garage. Robbie and Harry joined them. 'Morning Ben, Harriet.' They shook hands warmly.

Robbie and Harry dragged a couple of the old tractors out for Ben to inspect, and Harriet and Nik found another old kitchen dresser, falling apart, but stacked with old china; platters, cups and saucers, mismatched pieces, some quite lovely.

By eleven-thirty they had another small pile of stuff to keep and a stack for the second-hand store. Ben made an offer on the old tractors and farm equipment, saying he had a couple of buyers for those. Nik took Ben and Harriet into the back bedrooms of the downstairs section of the house, showing them the chest of drawers; the dresser, plus the wrought iron lacework they would use on the cottage veranda, while Robbie and Harry brought the few extra pieces including the tableware, in for safe-keeping.

Lucy had set up a folding table on the house veranda, with checked tablecloth, and laid out the carrot cake, plates, lemonade, and glasses.

'You've got so much done already, Nik. Much quicker than I expected. And your ideas for the cottage and house are great. I don't think you will have any trouble attracting guests here. In fact, you're such a success story for my own endeavours, bringing folk here for a permanent tree-change, I'd love to recommend your accommodation when I have buyers in the area needing somewhere to stay for a few days. Seeing how well you're doing will make my job,' Harriet turned to Ben and smiled, 'and Ben's so much easier. You're a walking advertisement.'

Nik happily agreed. Seeing the bathroom taking shape in the cottage, with all the old tiles and fixtures pulled out, had created a blank canvas and she was eager to start putting it together. 'I'll set a launch date, Harriet. Wondering if I should hold an event, you know, a morning tea or something out here for locals to see it.' She nibbled her bottom lip. 'And I need to find someone to help with a marketing strategy, a website, social media, publicity. I know a little bit about such things, but I'm no expert.' She sighed, 'I'm an accountant, we're not usually known for our creativity.'

'Oh, I don't know Nik. You might be selling yourself short. But Harriet can give you some guidance.' Ben cleared his throat. 'And there is a woman just up the road we can introduce you to. She's a graphic artist. Did the design work for our new branding.' He inclined his head toward the signage on his vehicle.

Looking over at the signs, Nik admitted the branding was eye-catching. 'Okay. All recommendations gratefully accepted, thank you.'

Robbie and Harry had returned to the cottage, close to finishing the bathroom walls while Lucy wandered off to see the puppies.

Walking Ben and Harriet to their car, Nik thanked them for coming out. Graeme from the second-hand shop was arriving the next day and would pick the tractor pieces up for Ben at the same time. Standing with Harriet for a moment before she stepped up into the car, Nik said quietly. 'Thank you, Harriet. I'm so glad I responded to your marketing message. This move is already working out better than I hoped. Especially for Lucy.'

Harriet gave Nik a warm hug. 'This place has a way of getting to you Nik. I was just passing through more than a year ago, when a mishap with my car left me stranded for a bit. Best thing that ever happened to me.'

Waving them off, Nik felt a lightness in her shoulders and an unfamiliar feeling in herself. She analysed it as she strolled back to the house. It was happiness. She was feeling happy. For the first time in almost a year.

~

THE WORK ON THE BATHROOM WAS LARGELY FINISHED, BUT ROBBIE, and sometimes Harry, turned up most days, sanding back the floorboards inside and around the deck. The new bathroom fixtures were due in at the end of the week when the plumber would come back to install them. The boys had put in a basic kitchenette, the cupboards had a heritage look and Nik and Lucy decided on the final colour scheme, buying the paint from the local hardware store.

Mid-week, on the way back from town, Nik pulled into the little Barrington Public School. It was school holidays and empty, but they had a walk around and peered through the windows of the three classrooms. 'Do you think you'd like to come here, Lucy, at the start of term? I had thought to keep home-schooling you, but Harry went to this school and said he loved it. It has about sixty students and only three teachers. Not big at all.'

Lucy didn't answer straightaway, but she walked around thoughtfully, pointing out the tennis court and playing field to one side of the buildings and the library now in the original old schoolhouse. A sign proudly declared the school was established in 1864. 'Look, Mum, gosh, it's really old.' She turned around in a circle, taking in the small, neat campus. 'I think I'd like to come here. Is this really where Harry went to school?'

'It is. I think Robbie went to school here too. And his father. What do you think?'

Tucking her hand into Nik's she leant against her briefly. 'Well … I've still got a year before High School. If I start here next term, I might make some friends to go to high school with later.' This was said with a firm little nod of her head. Nik squeezed her hand lightly. 'Good idea. That's a really positive way to look at it. I'm proud of you.'

ON THURSDAY MORNING A LARGE TRUCK PULLED IN, UNLOADING all the bathroom fixtures. Lucy watched from the veranda as Nik directed the burly delivery men to place everything just inside the main room of the cottage. Harry had gone to Rawden Vale for the day to finish work on a fence and Robbie said he would be at home working with his young horses, but to call him if they needed help unloading.

Everything was out of the truck inside an hour, with Nik choosing not to disturb Robbie who had been at his own place so little in the last three weeks.

Robbie had advised the plumber, Brendan Baxter, that the fixtures would be delivered and expected him to come over the next day to begin installing them.

15

T he plumber's van arrived that afternoon and as Nik walked across to speak to him, she secretly wished he hadn't come until the next day, as Robbie had requested, when he would be there too. She really didn't like the way he looked at her.

Baxter was already in the cottage, unwrapping the new bath.

'Hi Nik. Thought I'd get a start on this. You've chosen some great quality pieces.' He smiled at her, but she saw his eyes rove over her body as he did.

Looking directly at him, she stepped into the room. 'Thank you, Brendan. Good bathrooms seem to attract guests. I'm pleased with what we've chosen too.' She was standing by the large claw foot bath, deep and wide, big enough for two, it would take pride of place in the new bathroom.

He stepped closer to her, stroking the edge of the bath. 'Oh yes, this is a beauty. Who wouldn't love to take a soak in this one, especially with a sexy woman?' He winked at her as he spoke. 'Perhaps we should take it for a test run, once I've got it installed.' Nik took a step back.

'That won't be happening.' Turning, she walked to the door. 'I'll leave you to your work.'

'Aw, don't be like that. You're an attractive woman, living here by yourself. You must be missing a little male company.' He walked toward her. 'I'd be happy to help you out, if you know what I mean.'

With her heart suddenly racing, Nik tried to remain calm. 'I'm paying for your plumbing services, Mr Baxter. Nothing else.'

She stepped outside and closed the door firmly, but not before she heard him snarl, 'Bitch. Who do you think you are?'

She fled across to the house, pulling out her phone to call Robbie. As she reached the veranda, she slowed down, the phone in her hand. She shouldn't call Robbie. Baxter was a tradie and sometimes they could be a bit rough. She should learn to handle men like him, not let them frighten her. She slid the phone back into her pocket but stayed by the house all afternoon.

When the plumber's van drove out, she walked across to the cottage to see what he had achieved. She had to admit his work was good. All the pieces, except the large bath, were in the right place, and he had some of the connections and taps on too. She knew it would take two men to lift the bath in, but also knew Robbie wanted to tile the floor first. Sighing, she closed the door. He'd only be here a couple more days, then they would use Robbie's regular plumber when they started the renovations in the house.

NIK HAD THE NIGHTMARE THAT NIGHT, FOR THE FIRST TIME IN THREE weeks. Her ex-husband Patrick had been standing with his new wife, holding his baby in one arm, pulling on Lucy's hand with the other. Nik was pulling on Lucy's other hand and they were tugging so hard Lucy was crying out in pain. Just as Nik was about to give up, let Patrick take her, he morphed into HIM. The other one. Michael. Her big mistake. Michael was huge, he grew larger in her dream, knocking Patrick out of the way with a sweep of his hand. Sneering, he yanked Lucy to his side. His massive hand, a fist now, came for Nik. Hitting her in the ribs, then, once again on her feet, when she rushed to get Lucy. Pain swept through her and she tried again and this time his fist connected with her head, his ring slicing her open. Blood in her eyes, she screamed for Lucy, but he pulled her away. As he grew larger, Lucy seemed to shrink, until Nik could barely see her.

Waking in a cold sweat, Nik rushed to Lucy's room. She was asleep, curled up with a book about dogs lying beside her. It was a book Robbie had loaned her, about training a working dog. Climbing into bed beside Lucy, Nik curled up and eventually fell asleep.

'Mummy?' She opened her eyes. Lucy was facing her. She reached out and pushed Nik's hair back from her face. 'Are you okay, Mum? Did you have the nightmare?'

Blinking once or twice, Nik nodded. They studied each other. Nik noticed Lucy was more 'present', less inclined to disappear inside herself. Even asking the question was a sign of her growing confidence, and maturity.

'Why, Mum? Why did you have a bad dream?' Nik shook her head, not wanting to mention the plumber, not wishing to scare Lucy, or God forbid, set her back.

'I guess it just popped into my head while I slept. I'm fine, really. I hope you didn't mind me coming in here to you.'

Lucy snuggled closer. 'I don't mind. But we are getting better, aren't we? Remember how in the beginning, we always slept together. We needed each other 'cos of the bad dreams.' She patted Nik's shoulder. 'But I haven't been having the bad dreams at all. Lately I just dream about horses and puppies.' She giggled and Nik smiled, relieved.

'Good. Let's get up, have a juice, then check on the puppies and feed the horses. Do you think we could go for a ride together, along Robbie's paddock and back?' Nik stretched.

Lucy was out of bed as Nik spoke, pulling on her jeans and hunting around in a drawer for clean socks. 'Yes! Let's do that. We can have our ride before Cowboy Dad gets here. Won't he be surprised?'

Laughing, feeling better, Nik got out of bed. 'I'm going to get dressed, then race you downstairs.'

'You're on!'

Pulling on the faded jeans she now thought of as her 'riding jeans,' Nik added a sleeveless cotton shirt and ran a brush through her hair before running downstairs, boots in hand, right behind Lucy.

Scout wagged her tail when Nik opened the laundry door, standing and letting the puppies roll away from her as she stepped outside. Lucy filled the water bowl and gave all the puppies a pat, with a generous cuddle for Minnie, while Nik changed their bedding.

It was only just after dawn and Nik felt a growing sense of confidence and peace as she nudged Honey into a trot, then canter, Lucy beside her on Diana, as they rode in the direction of Robbie's place. Nik had not been this far, and she was curious about his farm and house. Lucy had ridden this way with Robbie a couple of times and knew the way. Navigating into another paddock, she saw the farmhouse in the distance. A single level timber home with a high roofline and two chimneys.

Looking at her watch, Nik slowed her mare to a walk. 'We should head back now. Robbie is probably on his way over in his ute.'

'Okay.' Nik was careful to walk on the way back as Robbie had warned her the horses may try to break into a gallop when heading home.

Nik noticed the plumber was already at work as they hitched the horses. She unsaddled while Lucy brushed them down. Nik frowned and looked at her watch. Robbie and Harry hadn't arrived yet. They were usually here by now.

Back in the house, Nik checked her phone. Robbie had sent a text.

Will be late today, sorry. Vet coming to look at injured horse. Harry still at other job. Call me if you need anything.

Nik nibbled on her lip while she looked at the phone. She would prefer Robbie to be here to deal with the plumber, but if he had an injured horse of course that would take priority. She messaged back.

All good here. See you later. Hope horse is ok.

Upstairs, buttering toast, she told Lucy that Robbie would be late, and Harry was at the other job. Lucy nodded, then announced she was going to sit with the puppies and study the dog training book.

Laughing, Nik said, 'they haven't even opened their eyes Luce, I think they're a bit little for training yet.'

'I know, but I'm just going to read about it anyway. And

Scout likes me to be there.' Nik nodded. Lucy was happy, relaxed. That's all that matters.

Nik chose not to go over to the cottage; the bloody plumber could just get on with it. She didn't want to give him another chance to leer at her. She showered quickly and changed from her riding gear into beige capri pants and a sleeveless top. Checking it didn't show any cleavage, just in case Baxter came to the house, Nik went into her downstairs office and began answering emails and responding to client requests.

Mid-morning, she saw Lucy out with the horses, brush in hand. She shook her head. They'd be the best-groomed horses in the district.

Heavy footsteps on the veranda broke her reverie. Nik stood, pushing her chair back. Stepping toward the open door, Baxter loomed in the entrance, his bulk blocking out the light.

'Do you need anything?' Nik knew her tone was cool, but she didn't want to give him any encouragement to be fresh with her. She hoped Lucy was still in with the horses and out of earshot.

He leaned against the doorjamb. 'There's no need to take that tone *Nik*.' He straightened. 'I'm sure we can be friends.' He towered over her, and she was tall. But she held her ground although her voice was dripping with tension.

'Let me get this straight, *Baxter*. You are here to complete a plumbing job. Nothing more. You are deliberately trying to intimidate me. It's unprofessional and unnecessary and certainly won't lead to *friendship*.'

'You already giving it to Robbie Stewart?' His tone became more aggressive, and he took another step toward her. She prayed Lucy was out of earshot. 'Old Robbie hasn't had any since the beautiful Jess died. Still grieving.' He touched his crotch with one hand. 'But a woman like you. A woman like you could help a man get over his grief.'

Nik stepped back, drew herself up and straightened her shoulders. 'You're a bully and a creep. And you're fired. Bill me for the work you've done.' She was almost shouting now but needed to keep momentum. 'Pack up your tools and get off my property!'

'You heard the lady.' This came from behind Baxter. It was said quietly, but with murderous intent. Robbie stood on the veranda, feet apart, body poised for a fight.

Baxter swung around. He was bigger than Robbie but seemed to deflate. 'It was just a joke mate. Chick can't take a joke.' He swaggered, stepping towards Robbie.

'Get your tools and piss off, Baxter. Don't make me say it again.' Robbie stood firm, arms crossed, chin up. For a moment Nik thought Baxter would swing at Robbie, but he stepped to one side and walked toward the cottage.

Nik put a hand up to her face, trembling. Robbie stepped inside, wrapped his arms around her, holding her for a moment. Releasing her, he stepped back as the van sped down the driveway, kicking up gravel with its tyres.

'You did well, Nik. You held your own. I'd heard rumours about Baxter but had no idea he was a bully. And a sleaze. I'm sorry to have brought him onto your place.' He looked across at the cottage, a muscle in his jaw twitching.

'It's okay. I don't think he would have attacked me. All talk, I think. But he scared me.' She looked around. 'I hope Lucy didn't hear.' But she knew the conversation had become loud. Knew in her heart Lucy would have heard some of it. It suddenly became important to find Lucy, make sure she was alright.

'Lucy.' Nik looked at Robbie. She pushed past him and ran

around the veranda to the laundry, Robbie on her heels. Scout was there, with all the pups except Minnie. Outside, Nik looked around wildly, fear on her face.

'The horses! Diana is gone! Her saddle too!' Robbie yelled. 'Where do you think she'd go, Nik?'

Nik shook her head, panicked. 'Maybe your place. We rode that way together early this morning.' Moving quickly, Nik grabbed Honey's saddle.

Robbie put his hand on her arm. 'I'll go on Honey. I'll be faster. Call Harry, he should be home by now. He can watch for her from there.' He touched Nik's face, wiping her tears. 'She'll be okay. But you should stay here in case she comes back. In case she didn't go this way. Nik, you need to be here for Lucy.' Nik nodded, pulling out her phone. Robbie had the saddle on Honey, as Harry answered her call. She handed the phone wordlessly to Robbie, unable to speak.

'Lucy has taken off son. She might be heading towards our place on Diana. Baxter had words with Nik, we think Lucy overheard and was frightened.'

'The bastard!' Nik clearly heard Harry's response. 'I'll saddle Blackjack and start toward Nik's. We'll find her.'

Robbie handed the phone to Nik, leant in, and kissed her on the mouth, gently, then said firmly. 'We'll bring her home safely. Stay here.' He leapt on Honey and nudged her with his heels. She leapt into a canter, crossing the grassy flats swiftly.

Hand over her lips, Nik ran inside, checking all the rooms just in case. She knew Lucy was on the horse but had to do something. She went back to the laundry, the door wide open, her phone in one hand, the other stroking Scout as she peered down the paddock past the water trough, searching for a sign of her daughter returning.

The phone rang. Robbie. She answered hurriedly. 'Is she there. Have you found her?' Robbie's quiet, patient voice answered. 'Lucy's right here. With me and Harry. She's fine. Put the kettle on, we'll be with you in twenty minutes.'

Crying with relief, Nik patted Scout. 'They've got her, Scout. She's okay.' Scout licked her hand, thumping her tail.

Nik ran upstairs and put the kettle on. From the upstairs window she could see the three horses with their riders, walking back together. Downstairs, Nik ran out to the hitching rail, waving madly. Lucy waved.

Within minutes they were at the fence. Lucy slid off Diana and ran to Nik. Nik knelt, wanting to hold her daughter tightly, but Lucy stood back, smiling through her tears. Something was wriggling inside her tee shirt. She reached in and drew out the puppy, Minnie. 'Minnie needs to be with her Mum too. I have to take her in to Scout now.' She leaned forward, kissing Nik on the cheek, before climbing through the fence, heading for the laundry.

'Thank you. Where was she?' Robbie and Harry looked at each other. 'Almost to our place. She knew the way and would have got there sooner, but she didn't want to shake the puppy up too much.' This was from Harry. 'I'll go check on Scout and the pups too.' He strode off.

Nik looked at Robbie. 'Was it because of Baxter? The argument?'

'It was. But Nik, she said she came to get me, and Harry, because she knows she's safe with us. She came to tell us Baxter is not a good man and that you, Nik, aren't safe with him. Her fear for you was much stronger than fear for herself.'

Amazed, Nik shook her head. She slipped her arm through his as they walked towards the house, where Lucy and Harry were standing together, waiting for them. 'Let's make a pot of tea, Mum.' Lucy put her hand in Nik's as they walked upstairs together.

LATER THAT NIGHT, NIK SAT ON THE EDGE OF LUCY'S BED. ROBBIE had ensured Baxter had taken all his gear. Nik knew he had phoned the man, who insinuated Nik had led him on. Robbie had stopped him, saying firmly, 'There'll be no more work with me, Baxter. I'm recommending Nik make an official complaint. You might want to consider relocating. I can't imagine anyone will use your services once this gets out.' He paused. 'Better still, why not mend your manners. Your business, and social life, will surely improve.' While Nik didn't hold great hopes for Baxter to change his ways, she felt sure he wouldn't be back to bother her.

Stroking Lucy's hair, Nik asked if she wanted to sleep in her own room or would she prefer to sleep with her.

'It's okay, Mum. We're safe now. And Robbie told me you were really strong, and that man wasn't able to scare you.' There was pride in Lucy's tone and Nik didn't want to admit that Baxter had scared her, although she now realised that she had stood up to him and he was backing down when Robbie arrived.

'Remember the promise I made you, Lucy? That I will never let a man into our home again, to live with us. That I will keep you safe, always.' Nik watched as Lucy nodded.

'But Mum. I think you're wrong. I don't need that promise.' Nik sat back, confusion on her face as Lucy spoke earnestly.

'I rode to Robbie's place for you, not me. Not because I was scared, although I was, but because I wanted to protect you.'

'What do you mean, sweetheart?'

'I know no one will ever hurt me. I know you will always protect me. I wasn't really hurt last time, Mum. You were. You were hurt protecting me. Us. I've been afraid something will happen to you. Not to me. But I haven't been able to explain it properly.' She stroked Nik's hand as she spoke. 'I rode to Robbie's because I trust him. He's a good man. Harry is too, although he's silly sometimes. Robbie will protect both of us. He loves you, Mum.' She looked down at their clasped hands, then looked up, tears in her eyes. 'I think Robbie loves both of us. Like he loves Harry. I don't mind if he's here all the time. I like it when he's here. Harry too.'

Nik hugged Lucy close. 'I like it when he's here too, Luce. Harry too. I like it a lot. But first things first. Let's all be friends first, okay? If it works out, maybe one day we can be something more.'

Lucy muttered into Nik's shoulder. 'We can be a family one day. I think we can be a family.'

16

It was late March. Nik, Robbie, and Harriet were sitting on the veranda, waiting for Lucy to be dropped off by the school bus. Minnie, the puppy, was curled up on Nik's lap.

'So, she likes the school, Nik?' Harriet took a mouthful of scone, sighing as she did. 'That Lucy, she knows how to bake.'

Chuckling, Nik nodded. 'She loves it. She's topping the class in English, but Mrs Merrington told me last week that every story she writes stars at least one dog and several horses.'

Robbie laughed too, then poked Nik's arm. 'You know Lucy's trying to train this pup, and you keep picking her up and taking her on your lap. You're going to be in so much trouble if she sees you.'

Nik hastily set the puppy on the ground, its sharp teeth promptly latching on and chewing on Harriet's laces. Robbie threw the tennis ball under the plum tree and Minnie scampered after it.

'Tell me about this new idea you have for the accommodation Nik. It's gorgeous by the way, I love the cottage so much.' Nik followed Harriet's gaze toward the cottage, the beautiful rosewood doors standing sentinel, the wrought iron lacework painted white, wrapping around the whole building on the veranda.

'The cottage is exactly as we planned. Short term accommodation. We'd love to have your clients stay here when they're looking at relocating to this region.' She shot a glance at Robbie, who nodded. 'But we've changed our minds about the rooms downstairs in the house. There's now two bedrooms, a big bathroom, two living areas and a full kitchen.'

Harriet smiled, but her brow was creased as she considered this. 'Self-contained accommodation. That's good.' She nodded encouragingly at Nik.

'We aren't offering this to holidaymakers. Or house hunters.' The school bus had stopped, and Lucy was now running down the driveway, Minnie tearing toward her full pelt. Nik watched as Lucy knelt, the puppy leaping into her arms, licking her face while Lucy laughed with delight.

Turning back to Harriet, Nik said firmly, 'This accommodation is for women. Women who need it. Who need a place to go because they don't feel safe, or they have nowhere else to go. Or they just want a break. Women with children. Young mothers with babies. Women, girls, who have been through trauma.'

Harriet sat back surprised. A broad smile appeared on her face. 'Really? How wonderful! I love this idea. How can I help?'

Robbie spoke. 'That's not all. Nik and Lucy will offer the accommodation. Those that come can stay as long as they need to. They can help with the gardens, the vegetables. Cooking.

Servicing the cottage if they feel up to it. But we are also offering horsemanship lessons. To be with the horses, groom, feed and ride them. A sort of equine therapy. Harry and I will provide the horses.'

'And anyone staying in the cottage that wants to ride, or learn to ride, can have lessons too. Or just go for a ride with one of us if they have some experience.'

'Harriet, we hope you'll help with the marketing. Get the word out to the right places.' Nik rose to hug Lucy, finally at the house, Minnie at her heels.

'Hi Mum, Robbie.' Lucy gave him a peck on the cheek. 'Harriet.' She sat down, reaching for a scone. 'Has Mum told you our plans? It's a really good idea, don't you think?'

'I really do, Lucy. I'm thrilled to be included. I'll help as much as I can.'

Lucy stood, 'Have you seen the cottage yet, Harriet?'

Harriet rose. 'I saw it last week, but I don't think you had the final colour in the kitchen. May I take a look?'

'Sure. Come with me.' Lucy turned, smiling at Harriet. 'Minnie, stop it! Leave Harriet's laces alone.'

Nik stood beside Robbie, loving the feeling of warmth his arm around her shoulders generated. She picked up the puppy, which squirmed against her chest.

At the door of the cottage Lucy raised her eyebrows at Harriet. 'You know I'm getting a brother, don't you?'

Harriet glanced back at Nik and Robbie. It was common knowledge they were seeing each other. But no one had mentioned a baby.

Looking at Lucy, she said, 'Really? Is your Mum expecting a baby?'

Lucy snorted. 'No, silly. Harry. Harry's going to be my brother.' She opened the door and skipped inside.

THE END

AFTERWORD

While the town of Barrington does exist, it is little more than a village with a general store.

I've imagined elements of nearby larger towns, such as Gloucester, to create my version of the township of Barrington for this story.

Any similarities to people living or deceased, are purely coincidental and a product of my imagination.

The Barrington Tops, Bucketts Mountain, Rocky Crossing and Barrington and Gloucester rivers do exist – and it is a stunning region to visit.

ACKNOWLEDGMENTS

From the very first moment I envisaged an anthology with several Aussie authors, my go-to peeps for support and advice were Phil and Craig from Happy Valley. Can't thank you enough for your wisdom and introductions, and for supporting the industry as you do. @happyvalleybooks_read

This novella was originally released in the Love in a Sunburnt Land anthology - and my fellow writers - Leanne Lovegrove, Rhonda Forrest, Louise Forster and Emma Powell became much more than co-authors. We formed a writing and support group (unofficially) and we loved the experience so much that we've continued to meet, share and support each other. Oh, and we're working on Sunburnt Volume Two right now.

To Trudy Schultz of @destination_gloucester thank you for the stunning photography and local knowledge. Trudy provided the front cover image for this book - she puts out an annual calendar and owns and operates amazing accommodation in the Gloucester - Barrington region. If you want to visit the 'real' Barrington region, check out Trudy's insta.

Thank you also to Bloke for the music, laughter, love, omelettes and fancy schmancy seafood dinners. Couldn't do it without you.

And last but not least - my girls, Jas and Emi for your unwavering support and encouragement.

ABOUT THE AUTHOR

Susan Mackie is the author of Amazon best-selling novel *Charlie's Will*, the first in the Barrington Series. Book Two – *A Place to Start Over* has recently been released.

Susan writes romance novels filled with vibrant, authentic characters and a touch of mystery, set in Australian country towns. Oh, and there's often a horse or two, and maybe a dog, in her stories.

This is her first novella - written for the Love in a Sunburnt Land anthology. Susan also edits and publishes for other authors, under her *Small Town Publishing* imprint. Susan has two grown daughters and lives in Warwick, Queensland, with Bloke.

www.susanmackie.com

https://www.instagram.com/susanmackieauthor/

https://www.facebook.com/susanmackieauthor

https://twitter.com/susantyrrell1

ALSO BY SUSAN MACKIE

Charlie's Will – Barrington Book One

getbook.at/CharliesWill

A Place to Start Over - Barrington Book Two

getbook.at/APlaceToStartOver

Love in the Ragged Mountain Ranges has been lifted from - Love in a Sunburnt Land – Anthology. Five Aussie authors, five second-chance-love novellas.

getbook.at/SunburntLand